# THERE  MURDER

We entered t̶... ...̶ng was
immediately ... n be-
fore in the ho... ...n sud-
denly on the bed. All of the pictures here were
crooked, too. "Tony, do you remember that Mother
Goose rhyme—"There Was a Crooked Man?" I recited it to him before he could answer me:

> "There was a crooked man,
> And he went a crooked mile,
> He found a crooked sixpence
> Against a crooked style;
> He bought a crooked cat,
> Which caught a crooked mouse
> And they all lived together
> In a little crooked house."

Tony stared at me. Then he quickly straightened the
pictures. "All these tiny little crazy things . . . toy
mice and crooked pictures and leaf bouquets and
cats who vanish with nonexistent relatives. Don't
you see? It's all starting to come together. . . .

# A CAT IN
# WOLF'S CLOTHING

*An Alice Nestleton Mystery*

by
Lydia Adamson

A SIGNET BOOK

SIGNET
Published by the Penguin Group
Penguin Books USA Inc., 375 Hudson Street,
New York, New York 10014, U.S.A.
Penguin Books Ltd, 27 Wrights Lane,
London W8 5TZ, England
Penguin Books Australia Ltd, Ringwood,
Victoria, Australia
Penguin Books Canada Ltd, 10 Alcorn Avenue,
Toronto, Ontario, Canada M4V 3B2
Penguin Books (N.Z.) Ltd, 182–190 Wairau Road,
Auckland 10, New Zealand

Penguin Books Ltd, Registered Offices:
Harmondsworth, Middlesex, England

First published by Signet, an imprint of Dutton Signet,
a division of Penguin Books USA Inc.

First Printing, November, 1991
10  9  8  7  6  5  4  3

The first chapter of this book previously appeared in *A Cat of a Different Color.*

REGISTERED TRADEMARK—MARCA REGISTRADA

Printed in the United States of America

PUBLISHER'S NOTE
This is a work of fiction. Names, characters, places, and incidents either are the product
of the author's imagination or are used fictitiously, and any resemblance to actual
persons, living or dead, events, or locales is entirely coincidental.

# A Cat in
# Wolf's Clothing

# 1

*Why was the woman whispering?*

I had been in the Salzmans' apartment for about twenty minutes when I finally realized that Mrs. Salzman had whispered to me from the moment I entered. And that I had whispered back. The entire conversation was being conducted in whispers.

I was there to be interviewed for a cat-sitting job. Mrs. Salzman needed someone to visit her lonely feline three mornings a week while she was seeking medical treatment in a neighboring state. In other words, she would be sleeping elsewhere and her cat had to be reassured. The nature of the medical treatment was never mentioned, nor was the whereabouts of Mr. Salzman, if, indeed, he existed at all.

The cat's name was Abelard.

When the cat's name was revealed to me, I had a sudden insight that Mrs. Salzman was quite mad ... that her cat had been surgically altered and the poor woman was caught in a delusion that her cat had been altered for love of Heloise. She was acting out a medieval castration romance. But the thought vanished as quickly as it had emerged; it was only one of my dramaturgical fantasies—an occupational hazard for actresses.

Mrs. Salzman kept whispering to me what a lovely cat he was.

The problem was—where was he?

I couldn't see him.

"He's very frightened of people," Mrs. Salzman said, which was the first rational reason she had presented for this whispering.

Mrs. Salzman lived in a very confused apartment on East Thirty-seventh Street in Manhattan. The furniture, and there was a lot of it, lined the walls like a military procession. Abelard could be under any one of the pieces.

If I couldn't see Abelard, maybe I could hear him. Maybe I could hear his movements. Maybe that was another reason she kept whispering ... so as to be aware of Abelard's movements.

"I am so happy to be able to deliver Abelard to a real professional cat sitter," Mrs. Salzman whispered.

I burst out laughing, very loudly. I couldn't help myself. Mrs. Salzman drew back, shocked, her hand involuntarily smoothing her hair. She was an impeccably dressed woman except for garish green leather shoes.

It was impossible to explain to her why her remark had collapsed me into laughter. But only two hours before I had entered Mrs. Salzman's Murray Hill apartment, I had been reading a short squib about myself in the neighborhood newspaper *Our Town*. The anonymous "People" columnist had mentioned me as a neighborhood resident and noted that: "The stately, long-haired, still-beautiful Alice Nestleton is one of our finest little-known actresses . . . little known because of her penchant for obscure roles in obscure off-off-off Broadway plays."

The anonymous columnist then went on to add: "Alice Nestleton has long been a cult heroine to theater buffs."

The comment was absurd. Where were these "buffs"? In the supermarket on Third Avenue? I never met them.

Anyway, the whole point about that ludicrous description of me in the newspaper was that it *didn't* make me laugh. But it laid the groundwork. And when Mrs. Salzman characterized me two hours later as a "real professional cat sitter," the cumulative effect made me laugh out loud, heartily, raucously.

Mrs. Salzman quickly forgave my outburst and took me on a brief tour of her convoluted apartment. She pointed out the location of the cat food and the watering can for the plants and the lists of emergency numbers and several other key locations and objects.

There was still no sign of Abelard.

"What kind of cat is Abelard?" I asked.

"A lovely cat," replied Mrs. Salzman, thinking I was asking about his disposition rather than his breed.

"What color is Abelard?" I persisted.

She paused, cocked her head, and smiled. "Mixed."

"Mixed what?" My question came out a bit testy.

She ignored that question and led me into one of the hallways. "There are your three envelopes," she said. They lay on a small elegantly carved French cherrywood table.

"One for each day you'll be cat sitting next week," Mrs. Salzman explained. She picked up one of the envelopes and opened it—I could see there was a single hundred-dollar bill inside.

My God! Three envelopes! Three hundred-dollar bills! For three visits of about forty-five minutes each to a cat I hadn't even seen yet and might never see! Was this woman mad? It was a truly exorbitant rate of pay. Unless of course . . . unless there were problems associated with Abelard that she hadn't disclosed.

I was about to ask for a modest reduction in pay when Mrs. Salzman suddenly and dramatically put her finger against her lips, urging silence.

Had she heard Abelard? Was the mysterious cat about to emerge from the shadows?

We waited. Mrs. Salzman closed her eyes and seemed to go into an anticipatory trance. What a strange woman she was: gray hair; thin, serious face; tall, with a stoop at the shoulders; the very slightest hint of an Austrian accent clinging to her whispers; an abstracted manner, as if she were very far away.

4

We waited. And we waited. And we waited. Where the hell was Abelard?

"Maybe we should call him," I suggested gently.

Mrs. Salzman opened her eyes in horror. I had obviously said the wrong thing.

"He does not like to be called," she said in a compassionate voice, as if, even though I was a professional cat sitter, I was suffering some kind of mild learning disorder.

"What *does* Abelard like?" I retorted a bit sarcastically.

The sarcasm passed blithely over Mrs. Salzman's head. "He likes flowers and fruit and fresh turkey and music and birds ..." She stopped suddenly in the middle of her hysterical list, a bit self-conscious. She smiled and led me to the door, telling me that Abelard wanted more than an employee—he wanted a friend.

I walked home quickly, thinking about *my* cats, Bushy and Pancho.

Granted, they were a bit peculiar. Bushy, the Maine coon, was no doubt one of the drollest beasts ever created. And Pancho, my stray rescued from the ASPCA, well, he was borderline psychotic—spending most of all day and all night fleeing from imaginary enemies.

But at least my cats were visible! Not like Abelard. And my cats obviously had a grudging affection for me.

I climbed the stairs quickly. Thinking about Bushy and Pancho always made me miss them fiercely—even though I had been away from the apartment for less than two hours.

"Alice! You're finally home!"

I stopped suddenly and peered up the badly lit landing toward the voice.

It was Mrs. Oshrin, my neighbor, the retired schoolteacher.

She was standing at the top of the landing. On either side of her was a very dangerous-looking man.

Kidnappers? Rapists? Junkies? Neighborhood derelicts?

I panicked. I turned sharply on the stairs and started to run back down to seek help.

"Alice!" I heard her call out. "Wait! There's nothing wrong!"

I turned back, confused, still frightened.

"They're police officers, Alice! They want to see you—not me!"

I waited, tentative.

"It's all very hush-hush," Mrs. Oshrin pleaded, as if that was an explanation. There was something about the way she used that very old-fashioned phrase—"hush-hush"—that sent an anticipatory tingle along my spine. But it wasn't fear.

# 2

Mrs. Oshrin brought them to my door as I fumbled with the keys. Obviously they had originally rung the wrong bell.

One was a short thick man with bright red hair who introduced himself as John Arcenaux; a detective with the Manhattan district attorney's office.

His companion was taller, a wiry bald man—his name was Harold Rothwax and he was a detective with the Manhattan South Division of the NYPD, temporarily assigned to a special unit.

They entered nervously. Both were wearing bluish suits and reddish ties, although the styles and shades varied.

The moment we were all inside, Rothwax said, "Detective Hanks has spoken highly of you."

So it was Hanks, my old friend/enemy, who had been a perpetual problem during that bizarre case of the aged Russian émigrés from the Moscow Art Theater who had taken to smuggling diamonds to enhance their life-styles in an alien land along with their strange white cats.

Mrs. Oshrin excused herself, smiling cryptically at me. The moment she left, the detectives became very nervous. I don't think they knew how to proceed with this tall, thin actress with the long golden-gray hair, dressed in an almost floor-length Virginia Woolf dress with gathered shoulders. But I knew they were there for my help, so I could afford to be benevolent.

"Won't you sit down?" I offered formally.

They sat carefully on the sofa, eyed by Bushy, who was lying regally on the rug and swishing his tail lethargically, or was it contemptuously. They sat as if I was about to serve them poisoned coffee—which I wasn't.

Arcenaux looked around the room intently and then said, "We need your help. Did you read about the Fourteenth Street murders?"

"The two brothers?"

"Yes."

I had indeed read everything I could find in the papers about them. It was very sad. Two brothers, both in their sixties and unmarried, who lived together in a new high-rise on Fourteenth Street. They were both recently retired city workers—one in the Department of Parks and the other in the Fire Department. They had been shot to death by a burglar. The police had apprehended a suspect. The brothers had lived with a beautiful Siamese cat who had not been harmed at all. The cat's picture had been in all the papers.

"But I've forgotten their names," I said.

"Jack and Arthur Tyre. Anyway, we arrested and charged a kid, Billy Shea, who works at the local supermarket. But it now turns out that all the kid did was rob the apartment after the brothers had been murdered by someone else."

He stopped and looked at Rothwax as if soliciting his colleague's help in soliciting my help.

Rothwax stood up and walked around the sofa, behind Arcenaux.

"May I call you Alice?" he asked.

"Of course," I said, though I'd be damned if I was going to call him Harold.

Something struck me very funny; I was in a drawing-room comedy; these men were investigating something absurd. The two detectives continuously shot quick glances at each other. It was as if they had been forced to visit me against their best judgment. And now that they were in the den of the cat woman, me, they were confused as to what was real and what was theater; they were confused about who I was and why they had been sent to seek my help.

Rothwax continued: "Let me get to the point. Over the past dozen or so years we've had a helluva lot of unsolved homicides. But we now believe that seventeen of these homicides were committed by a single individual—the one who murdered the Tyre brothers."

"A serial killer, as the movies say, Miss Nestleton," Arcenaux noted, "or a mass murderer. Either name would fit."

Rothwax continued: "We have never run across anything like this before because in every one of the cases, the mode of the murder was different. Each homicide was different in regards to weapon. The murderer killed seventeen times, differently."

I was confused. "Then how do you know it was the same person?"

"In each of the homicides there was no forced entry, and the victim owned at least one cat, and that cat was not harmed."

"A lot of people live with cats," I replied skeptically.

Rothwax leaned forward urgently, conspiratorially. "You see, we found something at the scene of the murders which, for the first time, ties them all together."

"Something?" I mimicked.

"We'd like to show this 'something' to you. We want your opinion. Detective Hanks says you're very sharp. And very knowledgeable about cats."

Pancho whizzed by and both men flinched. I laughed out loud.

"He moves fast," I said. They nodded.

"Now," Rothwax said, "can you go with us now?"

For the first time I truly sensed and believed the urgency in his voice.

"Why not?" I replied. The detectives smiled. Or were they grimacing? I looked at Bushy, who was now giving me one of his aloof treatments—staring either a million years back in space and time or a million years forward. That strange tingle came over me again—the one that had so mysteriously emerged after Mrs. Oshrin characterized the visit by the detectives as "hush-hush." But now the tingle itself could also be character- ized. I was tingling like I always did when I landed a part ... a role ... a juicy but difficult portrayal. I had slipped into the most prevalent delusion of the aging, perpetually out-of-work ac- tress—confusing anything and everything with a role ... the delusion of an always struggling ac- tress who had hitched her fading star to a kind of theater of the absurd—to a kind of stretching of the theatrical envelope that simply no longer existed.

But this was a murder investigation—not a role! It was something that had to be remembered. Just as I sometimes had to kick myself to remem- ber that Bushy was not a cat-sitting client ... he was my cat.

# 3

The Tyre brothers had lived in a very large wraparound studio on a very high floor of their Fourteenth Street building, which stood just west of Fifth Avenue. The wall-less kitchen was in the geographical center of the apartment. Two small bathrooms were set in the short hallway which led from the door to the studio proper.

The rest of the apartment was just space, shelves, a few pieces of minimal furniture, and windows—my, what windows!—covering all the walls on three sides. Just standing in the apartment was a wild, visual, urban ride. I sat down on a chair in front of the sections of windows which looked south. I could see the Twin Towers. I could see all of the downtown area. A gentle spring breeze rustled the blinds and raced through the apartment. It was not the kind of apartment one would expect to be rented by two recently retired sixty-year-old middle-class bachelors.

"There is where the bodies were found," Arcenaux said, gesturing to a spot not far from where I was sitting. "No struggle. None at all.

Just two .44-calibre slugs from a Colt. One in each brother. At the base of the skull. Execution."

"Clean, very clean," Detective Rothwax added.

I closed my eyes and let the breeze swell against my face. Sitting in that high apartment was like riding a roller coaster. Maybe there were too many windows.

"Madam . . . your mouse," a voice said.

I opened my eyes quickly and saw Detective Arcenaux mimicking a waiter.

He was holding a tray and bending over in a dramatic bow.

On the otherwise empty tray was a mouse! A mechanical one!

"Well? Look at it!" Rothwax ordered.

I picked the strange little mouse up from the tray Arcenaux offered me. It was one of those small windup mice. The skin and whiskers were some kind of fabric.

I wound it up and released it back onto the tray. It careened wildly from side to sight for a short time and then stopped dead in its tracks. Not at all like the economy of motion of a real mouse.

"At first," Arcenaux explained, "we thought it had been purchased by one of the brothers. But no one we questioned ever saw it in their apartment."

I picked the mouse up from the tray again. Poor little mechanical mouse, I thought. So sad.

Arcenaux continued: "Then, for no reason at all, someone ran it through the computer. The computer told us that in fifteen other murders there had been mouse toys inventoried at the scene of the crime."

Rothwax interrupted with his own thought. "Now, you may be thinking that wherever a cat lives in a household ... there will always be mouse toys."

"I was thinking along those lines," I admitted.

"Well, then, Miss Nestleton, I mean Alice, tell me—do you have a mouse toy in your apartment?"

"No."

"And, in fact, most cat families don't have mouse toys."

Arcenaux made a gesture with his hand, dismissing his partner's interruption as irrelevant.

"So now we have seventeen murders linked by a toy mouse of some kind found at the scene of the crime, along with the victim's cat or cats. No two of the mice are exactly alike—all are either windup toys or stuffed likenesses or plastic likenesses."

I laid the sad little toy mouse back down on the tray, feet up. It was becoming sinister.

"Tell her about Retro," Rothwax said to Arcenaux.

"You tell her," Arcenaux retorted.

"What or who is Retro?" I pressed.

"Well, its real name is Major Case Retrospectives," Rothwax explained. "It's a special new interdepartmental task force put together to deal with major unsolved crimes in the metropolitan area. It meets three mornings a week. We'd like you to attend." He paused and then added: "As a consultant."

I didn't respond at first. I started mentally listing all words that I knew beginning with retro: retrorocket, retrograde, retrospective, retroactive ... not many at all.

"Where is the cat?" I then asked.

"What cat?" Rothwax replied.

"The Siamese cat who lives here."

"Relatives took him," Rothwax replied.

"Well? Will you become part of Retro?" Arcenaux got back to the point.

Why would a murderer give his victim's cat a mouse toy? So strange! "Of course," I replied to the detectives, "I'll attend as many meetings of Retro as you wish me to attend. I want to help. I will try to help."

I stood up and started walking toward the door of the apartment. My eye caught a picture on the far wall—the north wall of the apartment.

It was odd that I had been sitting in that apartment for more than thirty minutes and I hadn't noticed anything on the walls. Of course, it was because the windows were overwhelming—the walls just a pathetic respite from the glass and the view.

My God! The painting was a print—of Van Gogh's painting *The Sunflower*. It was the same print that had hung in the kitchen of my grandmother's dairy farm in Minnesota.

I walked halfway across the large room—my

head suddenly filled with memories of childhood
... of seeing those wondrous Van Gogh yellows.
How many millions of farm children over the
years had watched those colors hung on their
grandmothers' walls? It was all so sad.

I walked closer. Something was wrong with the
print; it was crooked.

It hung crooked on the wall. That was all. I
closed the distance between myself and the wall
quickly and righted the frame. When I turned
around to walk back across the room toward the
apartment door, the two detectives were staring
at me.

Their stares were discomfiting. "The picture
was crooked," I explained.

The intensity of the stares didn't diminish.
What was the matter with them? Lusting?
Vengeful? Suspicious? Angry?

It was hard to tell. They weren't, after all, fe-
lines.

# 4

We were in the subbasement of a massive New York state courthouse building on Church Street in Lower Manhattan. The temporary home of Retro consisted of seven dark dismal rooms. Everything was old and thick and damp—dark wood, stained marble, massive oaken furniture, huge doors with old-fashioned brass knobs.

"And this is the computer room," Arcenaux said, ushering me into a high-tech fantasy. The room was filled with whirring cackling terminals and printers and phone lines. Several earnest-looking individuals in the room, working at their trade, ignored us.

"Any kind of information you need—they'll print it out for you," Rothwax said. He picked up a small blank slip from one of the desk trays and held it up for me to see.

"Just fill out what you want ... name of victim ... type of information sought ... they'll do any kind of computer search you want. Just sign your name and put your number on the slip."

"Number?" I was confused.

Arcenaux dug into his pocket and pulled out a small clip-on badge.

"You better put this on," he said. I stared at the small card: "ALICE NESTLETON. RETRO CONSULTANT. #106."

I pinned the card on above my right breast.

When I looked at them to signal I was ready to proceed, the two detectives averted their eyes. I was making them uncomfortable again. Maybe it was my dress—maybe they thought I had dressed inappropriately for my first appearance at Retro. I was wearing a dress I hadn't put on in more than ten years. It was a long, thin, flannel shift—white with red flowers around the shoulders. In fact, it looked suspiciously like a nightgown, with sleeves and all.

Why I chose it, I don't know. The last time I wore it was when I was still married—during a vacation in Southold on the North Fork of Long Island, where I spent days walking dreamily along the shore of Peconic Bay.

We headed toward the main reading room. Just before we entered, Rothwax said, "By the way, you'll be getting three hundred dollars a day as a consultant, plus expenses. I'll show you how to submit the vouchers later."

I nodded. What could I say? Between cat sitting for Abelard at one hundred dollars a morning and consulting for Retro, I was becoming independently wealthy.

Rothwax opened the door and walked in. I followed, Arcenaux behind me. There were about eight people in the room already, sprawled on chairs. It looked like an office that had been converted into a schoolroom. Rothwax pointed to several empty chairs by the window and started to thread his way there. We followed. Halfway to our seats I heard: "Meow."

It came from the front of the room. I froze. This kind of childishness was not what I had expected—not even from a group comprising primarily police officers.

I started to walk again toward the window chairs. This time the "meows" burst out all over the room and one voice even announced in a melodramatic roll, "The cat woman strikes."

I wheeled, furious. Arcenaux stepped between me and the seated antagonists. "Let it slide," he whispered, "please . . . this time let it slide. Boys will be boys."

"You mean cops will be cops," I retorted. He shrugged and led me to the window seat.

The moment I sat down I forgot all about the petty harassment because I found myself staring at the front wall, over the blackboard.

Seventeen large photos were hung there. Seventeen faces. They were mesmerizing. Below each photo in a large, almost childlike crayon writing was the name of the person in the photo . . . age . . . sex . . . race . . . occupation . . . mode of death.

I was looking at the reason I was there—seventeen murdered people.

I read the captions carefully.

Laura Elrauch. Waitress. 24. White female. Shot .22 long.

David Sprague. Physician. 54. White male. Throat cut.

Jill Bonaventura. 31. Unemployed. White female. Strangled.

Sekou Aman. 46. Writer. Black male. Shotgunned.

Louise Wu. 61. Nutritionist. Asian female. Poisoned (strychnine).

Patricia Saint-Rossy. 30. Police officer. Hispanic female. Strangled.

Jonathan Berger. 71. Retired chef. White male. Shot. .38 caliber.

Simon Baum. 66. Carpet salesman. White male. Shot. .32 caliber.

Sylvia Bonney. 43. Legal secretary. Black female. Bludgeoned.

Trent Apple Jr. 26. Unemployed. White male. Thrown from window.

Dennis Mulholland. 28. Computer programmer. White male. Knifed.

Harry Oakes. 77. Retired transit policeman. Black male. Shot. .25 caliber.

Joanne O'Dell. 37. Editor. White female. Shot. .32 caliber.

Shirley Wahr. 42. Department-store buyer. White female. Knifed.

Charlotte Koltay. 38. Junior high-school science teacher. White female. Shot. .25 caliber.

Jack Tyre. 63. Retired city worker, Department of Parks. White male. Shot. .44 caliber.

Arthur Tyre. 61. Retired NYC fireman. White male. Shot. 44 caliber.

It was so bizarre, sitting in that subterranean classroom, surrounded by men and women determined to find the killers of the people photographed. For a moment I couldn't care less about the killers. I wanted to do something for the dead. I wanted to ... Oh, how stupid it sounds. I wanted to resurrect them in their daily lives. I wanted to hear them laugh or weep. And I never knew one of them.

Arcenaux nudged me and pointed. A short stout woman with styled hair was striding into the room followed by a middle-aged gentleman with long eyelashes and a washed-out black turtleneck.

"That's Judy Mizener from the D.A.'s office. She's the head of Retro. She okayed you. The guy with her is one of the NYPD shrinks."

Judy Mizener stood in front of the desk and studied the audience. Her eyes caught my eyes and she smiled some kind of recognition. The photographs of the seventeen corpses stared at me from over her right shoulder.

"Well," she said to the assembled, "I hope you've all given a warm welcome to Alice Nestleton, who is going to be with us for a while. She'll bring a whole new perspective to the investigation, which is—and I remind you—going nowhere." She repeated the word "nowhere" very loudly and carefully as if dismembering it. Then she turned toward me and said, "We all look forward to your first presentation."

Presentation? I didn't understand what she was

talking about. Arcenaux picked up my perplexity. He whispered, "Everyone has to make short presentations. You just stand up and tell us your current thinking on the case."

Judy Mizener was now gesturing with her hand, and the turtlenecked man, who had been hovering in the background, stepped forward.

"And now I'd like to present Dr. Sam Jassy, who is going to make some interesting points."

Judy Mizener moved away from the desk and sat down in a chair. Sam Jassy turned for a short while to stare at the photographs that hovered above him; then he began his talk.

"To make a long story short, which my profession rarely does, no one has convinced me beyond a shadow of a doubt that these murders are connected.

"But if they are—and this Retro meeting wouldn't be taking place if we didn't believe they were connected—then there is no doubt in my mind that we are dealing with a psychotic.

"And since these crimes span a thirteen-year period, there is a good possibility that we are dealing with an individual who moves in and out of mental hospitals and other primary care facilities. You all know the routine. Acting out. Hospitalization. Medication. Stabilization. Release. Relapse. My guess is paranoid schiz."

He stopped talking and began to circle the desk. I realized he had an actor's sense of pacing. Then he continued.

"How do we know we are dealing with a psychotic? Two very strong reasons. First, no one has been able to come up with a rational motive for the crimes. There seems to be no reason why all those people were murdered. It seems to be random selection. And that is the surest sign of a psychotic personality.

"Second, and most important: from my point of view, only a psychotic would attempt to conceal himself by using a different murder weapon in each attack while at the same time leaving a more or less identical calling card at the scene of each attack—some kind of mouse toy."

He then threw up his hands and smiled. "That's it. That's all I have to say. Any questions?"

There were a lot of questions. But I wasn't interested. I let my eyes wander back to the photographs, lined up, I now realized, in order of their corpsehood. The first victims first . . . the last victims last.

I wondered what photo they would have used of me if I had been one of the victims. They had obviously just taken family snapshots and blown them up, trying to obtain the most recent one of each victim. That was probably what made the collage so eerie. It was like staring into a home movie on death . . . shot the night before. Well, there was no place for me up there—no one had taken a snapshot of me in a long time.

"How about a cup of coffee?" Arcenaux asked. Then he added: "These people can question Jassy for another five hours. It's their way to get cheap short-term therapy."

We slipped out of the room and made our way from the cavernous building. It was a warm enough day to have our coffee on the street, with plain stale doughnuts purchased from one of the vendors who lined the sidewalk in front of the parks which adjoined the courthouse buildings.

"Well, what do you think?" Arcenaux asked.

"About what?"

"About Retro. About what you heard."

"I don't know how to answer that. I'm still a little flattered, a little frightened."

"I saw you staring at the photographs," he said, dunking the doughnut into the coffee. What an old-fashioned way of eating a doughnut. He suddenly became much less distant.

"Did you ever read *The Good Soldier,* a novel by Ford Madox Ford?" I asked him.

"No."

"It starts out with a line: 'This is the saddest story . . .' That's what I was thinking about when I looked at the photos. Just the sadness of it all . . . the incomprehensible sadness."

"You'll never make it as a cop," Arcenaux replied.

"I don't intend to."

"Sadness? What the hell is sadness? You sound like an actress now."

"I am an actress," I replied.

He nodded once, vigorously, and flung his remaining coffee into the street. "Actually the only sad thing about my life is that I couldn't make a go of it as the owner of a trucking firm. I liked to drive trucks from point A to point B. But that's a different kind of sadness ... isn't it?" He grimaced. "Let's get back."

# 5

It was six-thirty in the morning. I was sitting at my small kitchen table sipping half a cup of Medaglia d'Oro instant coffee, black with sugar, and staring up at Pancho. He was resting for the moment from one of his lunatic runs to escape imagined enemies—on the very top of my high kitchen cabinet. There he crouched, staring down at me, rust-whiskered, yellow-eyed, his scarred gray body mimicking some panther.

One could imagine his tail switching ominously ... if he hadn't lost most of it in some undocumented tragedy as a kitten.

"You know, Pancho," I said to him, "now that I have all this money coming in, I can buy you a replacement tail ... a prosthetic device. No one will ever know. Believe me, Pancho, they can do wonders nowadays."

He appeared uninterested.

"If you had a tail, Pancho, you'd probably get along better with Bushy. You'd have something to talk about."

Still no response.

"Well, if you don't want a new tail, I can buy

you tons of saffron rice." It was, for some reason, his favorite delicacy.

I took another sip of the coffee, and when I looked up, Pancho was gone. He was a very hard cat to know ... but to know him ever so slightly was to love him ... to coin a cliché. I spend half my waking hours longing to catch Pancho so I can hug him.

It was time to dress for my first real day as a paid NYPD consultant. I had decided to visit Abelard in the late afternoon rather than the early morning.

What to wear? I had to be, this time, a little more than Alice Nestleton out of an Edwardian used-clothing store. I had to wear the character of a consultant ... which is ... who knows? I would be working with corpses and computers. And cats, of course, always with cats.

I giggled into my black coffee, remembering a theatrical story. A Hollywood producer once told Brecht that Charles Laughton was such a great actor he could hold an audience enraptured just by reading the phone book onstage. Brecht agreed, replying that the only audience Laughton would get for such a performance, however, was Peter Lorre—and Lorre would surely be enraptured. The joke being, of course, that Lorre was a notorious drug addict.

I don't know why I thought of that story or what it had to do with the way I should dress for my first day at the office. But it did, no doubt, subconsciously determine the fact that I ended up walking out of my apartment looking like Alice Nestleton.

Retro had assigned me an office adjacent to the computer room. It contained hastily assembled chairs (three), desk, and file cabinets (four). There was a locked phone on the desk. Obviously I wasn't being encouraged to call out.

On the truly immense aged steel desk was a pile of office supplies: yellow pads, ball-point pens, paper clips in three sizes, index cards, a paperback dictionary, Scotch tape in a dispenser, and a stapler. There were no windows, just vents. I sat down in my office for about ten minutes, just as a formality, then entered the bustling computer room to interrogate the machines.

Once inside, I grabbed a few of the white request slips and took them to a raised writing ledge along one wall to study and fill out. I knew the kind of information I wanted.

"Will you marry me?"

I looked up, startled, toward the source of that bizarre request.

A small, almost miniature man was directly to one side of me. He was tiny in height only; his chest, encased in a starched white shirt, seemed to be grotesquely muscled. His hair was brushed back with a vengeance and his face was wreathed in a threatening scowl. He wore a fat bright tie with an enormous stickpin in it. Beneath one arm he had a large blue looseleaf book.

"I beg your pardon," was all I could say.

"Will you marry me? The moment you walked through the door, I fell in love with you. Desperately, totally, insanely in love with you. You are beautiful. You are intelligent. You are mysterious. And I am single. So, I repeat: will you marry me?"

I laughed at his passionate but ludicrous proposal. "Let me think about it," I replied good-humoredly.

His response was not in kind. He retorted angrily: "Make up your mind now! I can't wait."

I stared at him. Was he insane? "Well, then, no," I replied, and turned all the way around to be free of him.

"Fine," I heard him say, "so now let's get down to work, Alice Nestleton, consultant extraordinary."

I turned back toward the strange little man. He bowed slightly. "My name is Bert Turk. Not Bert the Turk. Just Bert Turk. I am your resource adviser. And a very good one. But I am also a disbarred attorney with a felony conviction. A bad egg, as they say. So how is it that such a bad egg is working in the heart of the criminal justice system? Because Judy Mizener is a compassionate woman and she also knows I can milk more crime data out of a data base than any twenty nonfelons."

It was such an explosive nonstop speech that I didn't know what to say.

"In short, Miss Nestleton, what I am telling you is that virtually every bit of data you want has already been requested and retrieved by someone before you ... and it's all here."

He motioned to a small empty seating unit—the kind one sees in microfiche libraries, a chair with a three-sided wraparound desk—and then he dropped the large blue book onto the desk. It made an explosive noise.

"Seek and ye shall find," he said, and walked quickly away. What a relief it was to get rid of that strange Mr. Turk.

I opened the blue book, which was basically a compilation of printouts. It was very sobering indeed. Every one of my questions, which I had been so proud of formulating at the time, had indeed been answered regarding the seventeen victims.

There was essentially no deep life-style resemblance among the victims. They came from all walks of life, races, classes. What they did have in common was trivial. They all lived in Manhattan ... they all lived with cats ... they all had no criminal records except for parking violations ... they all participated in the city's cultural offerings—from movies to parks to museums.

The data on the mouse toys was much less extensive because it was only with the last two murders that a connection had been posed, and much of this information had been obtained years after the events.

But all data pointed to the fact that none of the victims' relations or friends, when contacted, could remember seeing such toys in the victims' possession prior to the murders. Yet the police at the scene of each crime remembered it in retrospect, even if it wasn't recorded at the time because it was so trivial. So someone must have put it there! Very few of the toys had been traced to the point of purchase ... and when traced, no information on the purchaser had been obtained—probably because it was such an inexpensive purchase: no credit cards were used.

And there was no correlation between the toys and the victims—between, for example, wooden mice and sex of victim ... windup mice and sex of victim—so the computer said.

There were dozens of reproduced verbatim reports and interviews with relatives and loved ones of the victims. They were riveting because they were conducted before the police knew the victims were part of a murder chain. And since in each case robbery was quickly ruled out, the detectives on the case had to probe for secret passions, secret vices, anything to explain the sudden death of the victim. In no case was that secret found.

I read them until lunchtime, then took a long walk on Centre Street, then went back to the blue book, trying to avoid Mr. Turk at all costs.

To my surprise, the cat data in the blue book was good. Page after page of tables showed that there was absolutely no pattern in the cats of the victims—no patterns and no correlations. The victims had all different kinds of cats, some purebred and some not, some purchased from breeders, some from pet stores, some adopted from agencies. There were Siamese, Persian, Manx, Russian blue, tabbies, shorthairs, and old-fashioned alley cats—males, females, neutered.

And all had quickly been adopted by relatives or friends after the murders—said the blue book in a decidedly uncomputerlike aside.

I slammed the blue book shut at 4:10 P.M. My head and my ego ached. Every question I had thought to ask the computer had been asked and answered.

"We could have been so happy together," I heard crazy Mr. Turk say. Then he reached over and grabbed the blue book away from me.

"The file is updated with new data every three days," he said, "and of course we are open to your requests," then added archly, "if you have any."

I walked out of the computer room without saying a word and was about to return to my office when I suddenly felt the desire to see those photographs again.

The classroom was empty and dark. I switched on the light. Seeing them again like that, suddenly, from darkness to light, took my breath away. I sat down. How beautiful and peaceful they all looked in their chronological order of death. How odd it was that they were up on the wall only because of a mouse toy found where and when they died. The thought upset me. The more I thought about it, the more horrendous it seemed—their repose seemed to vanish. It was as if their sacrifice had been trivialized by the mouse toy. What sacrifice? To whom? I was beginning to think like a minister or priest. I closed my eyes and tried to nap.

"Abelard ... oh, Abelard ... Come out, come out wherever you are. It's me, Heloise ... your true love."

For twenty minutes I had been calling and crawling and groping amidst the furniture, peering over and under and between. He was there. I could hear him. I could hear him evading me.

I now believed beyond a shadow of a doubt that Mrs. Salzman was mad, that she had filled her apartment to the brim with totally inappropriate furniture in order to give her cat more room to hide.

Unable to coax him out or chase him down, I finally began to run through the entire lexicon of "dirty tricks" used by cat sitters since time immemorial to make cats appear.

They included: opening of food cans; wrinkling aluminum foil; calling out to the cat in a foreign language; singing; standing absolutely still in a yogic-type trance, suspending all respiration and body metabolism (this sometimes piques a concealed cat's curiosity); and others too embarrassing to mention.

Abelard remained hidden. My frustration grew. It was bad enough accepting one hundred dollars for a brief visit—the least I could do was look at the cat, in person, to make sure he was well.

33

I decided to use my number-one cat-sitting trick to make a cat appear.

I sat down on a chair, closed my eyes, folded my hands demurely on my lap, and proceeded to mimic the low throbbing notes of a city pigeon resting in her nest on a high ledge ... the same throaty sound that has driven untold millions of apartment cats mad with frustrated blood lust as they stare out closed windows at the succulent prey—so near, yet so far.

Abelard did not appear. Angrily I called out to him, wherever he was: "Well, you'll never be adopted by anyone if something happens to Mrs. Salzman. You're too damn stubborn."

I stood up and started to make final preparation for leaving. But my movements were slowing down. Something was bothering me—something I had said to Abelard. I had threatened him with abandonment. He would not, I had told him, be adopted like the other cats. What cats? I was thinking about the sixteen cats of the seventeen victims who had all, the blue book told me, been quickly and readily adopted by relatives of the deceased.

Why had I believed that "fact"?

Because the computer told me.

Because I had been so flattered at being hired as a consultant for Retro that the flattery had overwhelmed my common sense.

*But* ...

If there is one great unalterable tragic fact of cat existence, it is that the hardest and most difficult task on earth is to find a new home for a cat who is not a kitten and who has lived in one home for a long time.

The computer had lied. The computer had been misled. The police had been hoodwinked. There was as much chance for all those cats to have been quickly and painlessly adopted by loving relatives as I would have winning the New York Marathon.

The extent of my gullibility made me cringe. I sat down again. At least now, I realized, I had the makings of my first presentation to Retro as a consultant. I had the correlation they had been looking for without success.

# 6

I stepped up casually. The room was full. Judy Mizener was sitting in the front seat. Near the small window sat Rothwax and Arcenaux. In the rear, near the door, was that bizarre little man Bert Turk. They all looked a bit bored, not knowing that their cat lady was about to drop an evidential bombshell into their self-assured policework.

I had planned my presentation as a theatrical event, a one-woman show.

I began gently, with an anecdote.

"A very famous and eccentric acting coach named Grablewski once made a speech to his students telling them that the real function of a good actor is to strip the stage of the junk the playwright burdens the event with. 'What is missing in a play,' he would say, 'is more important than what is there.' "

I waited a few moments to let the saying sink in and then proceeded.

"Let me project this onto our situation. What is missing in these murders is more important, I believe, than what has been found."

I looked around at their faces. Now they seemed puzzled as well as bored.

"Let me refresh your memories. Let me explain myself step by step." I was moving into my pedagogic role and enjoying it immensely.

"Each of the victims had a cat. After each murder the victim's cat was quickly adopted by a relative or friend of the deceased.

"At least that is what the computer records in the blue book.

"Obviously no one in Retro thought this information important enough to double-check. I did. All adoption reports on all the cats are hearsay. There is absolutely no validation whatsoever. No one has seen any one of those cats in its new home."

I paused and let that sink in. I could feel now that the audience was keying to my lines. I could feel their anticipation.

"In other words," I said, lowering my voice, "the only legitimate correlation we have, other than the mouse toys, is that all cats of all victims have vanished without a trace."

I smiled. "And to take this to its logical conclusion ... the vanished cats are not ephemera—they are the stuff of, and maybe the motives for, the crimes."

There it was—all laid out. Simple. Eloquent. Logical. Stemming from the facts we had and the facts we didn't have. I stepped back to field the furious questions and comments I knew would be coming my way.

There wasn't a sound in the room. I waited, shifting my weight uncomfortably. I heard a nervous shuffling of feet. The faces in the room looked away from me. They stared at the ceiling, at the floor, at each other. What had gone wrong?

Then Judy Mizener stood up. "Thank you, Miss Nestleton. We appreciate your comments." And she made a gesture with her hand signifying that I should sit down. I did so, uncomfortable, embarrassed, confused. I was not used to misreading an audience reaction so totally.

"Our next speaker," Judy Mizener said, "comes to us from the Federal Bureau of Investigation in Baltimore. As you know, they have a very sophisticated serial-crime unit down there and we have been sending a lot of our information to them. Chandler Grannis is here to report on some interesting developments."

A thin, impeccably dressed sandy-haired man stood and came to the front of the room. He was wearing a gray suit with a gray vest, a brown shirt and a brown tie. He opened the button of his jacket and the holstered weapon on his left side was clearly visible. He spoke with a soft Southern accent.

"It is an honor," he said, "to follow such a beautiful speaker. Miss Nestleton's theory is fascinating. It's sort of like saying that because Babe Ruth always visited brothels before a game, there was a correlation between the number of home runs he hit and the number of condoms he used."

The room exploded with derisive laughter. I flushed with anger and shame.

After the laughter came applause, then a dozen scabrous comments from the audience to the speaker, affirming his description of my theory as a condom analogue . . . and going even further. No one looked at me, but all their comments were directed at me.

The FBI man waited until the noise had died down and then turned for a moment to stare at the photographs of the dead on the wall.

When he turned back, the room was silent again.

"I am not going to pull my punches. From what I have seen of your investigation, you people are in outer space. Probably because there was no hint of any connection between all these murders until the last two, when you found the now infamous mouse. Do me a favor. Forget all this cat-and-mouse nonsense. Okay? You have a very ugly character to find. Okay?

"In fact, you people are so hoodwinked by the cat-and-mouse nonsense that you overlooked the basic pattern in these serial killings."

He paused and stared straight at Judy Mizener, who was now getting very uncomfortable.

He continued: "Me . . . I'm just an old-fashioned guy. So I came up with some old-fashioned facts. The kinds of facts that always hold up in these kinds of crimes—rhythm of the murders and times and sequences and dates."

He raised his hand toward the photos. "All of

them were murdered between December and June. The murders were usually sixty-two to sixty-five days apart in each given year when there were two murders in one year. Let me repeat. Murdered between December and June. Murdered sixty-two to sixty-five days apart."

Several people in the audience began to write his data down.

"So, what you have here falls into the very classic pattern of serial killers—numerological or astrological correlations of some kind. In short—a nut."

Agent Chandler Grannis grinned. He had finished his presentation. He had crucified me with scorn and showed everyone the power of the Bureau.

He buttoned his jacket and left the front of the room to be engulfed by admirers. I sat still. Slowly the room began to empty out. Once, the agent shot me a sheepish, almost apologetic glance. I glared back at him. The fool. He thought he had mocked me out of existence. Yes, the Babe Ruth/condom analogy had been powerful and destructive. But his subsequent comments had confirmed my theory. And he didn't even know it. No one in the room knew it but me.

Soon, only Judy Mizener and I remained in the room. She stayed where she was and I stayed where I was. The distance between us remained constant.

"Look," she said, "this is all very painful and embarrassing to me. I made a mistake in taking you on. A lot of the staff on Retro resent you. They don't know how to deal with you. They don't know what to make of you. They look on you as some kind of psychic ... as a nut. I'm sorry. But that's the way it turned out."

"Are you firing me?" I asked.

"Yes. I think that's what I'm saying. It would be foolish to keep you on, because you won't get any cooperation from the staff ... and it would be painful to you."

"Even though the FBI agent confirmed my theory?"

She stared at me, startled. Her reply was almost a shout: "Confirmed? Are you crazy? He made an ass out of you and your theory!"

I smiled cryptically. "I think not. You see—the December-to-June period of the homicides coincides with the normal breeding season of the cat in the Northern Hemisphere."

A cloud of confusion seemed to pass over her face. Then she stared at me and blinked. I let the other shoe drop on her resolve and her certainty.

"And the sixty-odd days between murders, when they occurred in pairs or triplets, correspond to the normal gestation time for the birth of kittens."

Judy Mizener started to pace back and forth. I could feel the questions racing through her head. Was this woman truly crazy? Was she brilliant? Did her interpretation of the agent's data have any relevance to the real world? Was this cat lady worth another shot even over the hostility and derision of the Retro staff?

She held up her hand. "Look, I don't know how to respond to what you just told me. Let's make a compromise. You stay in for the meanwhile, at half-pay and a low profile. I'll take you out of your office and assign you a small cubicle down the hall, with the same complete access to all data. Just don't show up for a while at the meetings until the uproar has died down. Okay?"

Ordinarily I would have refused such an offer immediately. No one could play a role with that kind of demeaning, halfhearted support. But this wasn't theater—and those seventeen photos staring at me over Judy Mizener's shoulder mocked the very idea of hurt feelings.

"Fine," I said. She smiled grimly and walked out.

I remained seated. It was obvious to me that no matter how long I remained with Retro, no matter the capacity, I could not depend on the other members of the group for help. And I surely needed help.

I turned suddenly around in my seat, no longer able to tolerate the gaze of those dead people. It was too sad. Too, too sad. I would have to call my friend Anthony Basillio the moment I got home. He would help. He always did.

# 7

There was no answer at Basillio's home in Fort Lee, New Jersey, that night. I called at six, eight, ten, and midnight. No answer. No answering machine. Where was he? Where were his wife and two small children? Had they moved? Were they on vacation? He never went on vacation.

If they had moved, Basillio would have contacted me. Granted, we hadn't been in touch with each other since our last adventure together with the murderous Russian émigrés and their strange white cats. But Tony Basillio would have contacted me if they had moved.

We were very old friends. We had, in a sense, both been crushed to death by theatrical longings and each had been ressurected in his or her own way.

Tony Basillio had left the theater with bitterness to open a successful chain of copier shops called Mother Courage—in honor of his beloved Brecht.

The only memory he held sacred was his critically acclaimed scenic design for a production of *St. Joan of the Stockyards* which ran for sixty-six days in a church in the West Village in the mid-1970's.

Basillio drank and gambled and did all kinds of crazy things, but his mind and heart were pure gold. He saw things that others didn't see—and he had proved to be invaluable when it came to criminal investigation. He was plugged into the world. Oh ... it was a wet, wiggy, dangerous socket—but he was plugged in.

Swede, he always called me, because I was from Minnesota. And all he needed was two drinks to begin lecturing me on my foibles as an actress ... my incomplete knowledge of theatrical history ... and on my avant-garde pretensions.

But where was he now?

The next morning I called all his Mother Courage copying shops. He wasn't there. They gave me vague answers. I kept leaving desperate messages that it was urgent for him to contact me. When I specifically asked his employees where the boss was, they double-talked.

Finally, at almost eleven in the morning, the phone rang and it was Basillio. Something was wrong. His voice was weary. He was, he said, in the Hilton, of all places, on Fifty-fourth and Sixth Avenue. I asked him what he was doing there. He didn't answer. Come over, he said. Now. I did. I took a cab.

He looked like he had been in that hotel room for weeks. He was thin, very thin, and agitated. His always bad complexion, the only thing that marred his very handsome face, was even worse. The ashtrays were full. The bed was strewn with aluminum foil from the junk food he had brought in. And the brandy bottle on the dresser was empty.

"I left my wife," he said. "I left my wife and two kids and I'm not going back. They can have every penny I got. Do you understand that?"

I sat down suddenly on the bed beside him. He jumped off the bed and began to pace, running his hands constantly through his long, swept-back gray-black hair.

"Do you know why I left them, Swede? And do you know why I haven't even gone into one of my stores for the last two weeks?"

"Calm down, Tony, you're shouting," I replied.

He glared at me. "Because the only thing that ever meant anything to me was the theater. Actors on stages. So I'm going back into it and I don't care if I starve to death. And I don't care if I spend the rest of my life designing stage sets that are never used, much less looked at. Do you understand, Swede? I'm forty-four years old. I'm going to die with a vision. Do you understand me, Swede?"

"Calm down, Tony."

He chopped one arm violently through the air. "Who the hell are you to tell me to calm down? You're a goddamn dilettante, Swede. A little off-off-off Broadway . . . a little cat sitting . . . a little crime solving."

His face went suddenly very pale. "Oh, Swede,

I'm sorry. I have a big mouth." He sat back down on the bed beside me. We both started to cry. Then we embraced.

Then something snapped in both of us. He started to kiss me passionately, as if we were twenty years younger ... and I responded.

Then we made love. There were no words. Few preliminaries. We just made love—wildly and desperately ... two middle-aged out-of-work theater people in a desperate room.

It was late afternoon. Shadows were beginning to appear on the carpet of the hotel room. Neither of us had spoken. We both seemed to be in shock from what had happened.

Finally Tony said, "Well, Swede, since I first met you, all those years ago, I've been trying unsuccessfully to seduce you—now you show up and seduce me."

"That's not what happened, Tony."

"What did happen?"

I didn't answer. I didn't know. We had both sort of lost control. It could not be explained. Middle-aged romantics. I stared at the carpet where I had hastily flung my clothes.

"Why did you come here, Swede?"

"I need your help, Tony."

"As you can see, I'm not much help to anyone now." His hand reached out and traced the profile of my face. "I've always loved you, Swede."

I didn't want to hear that. What had happened between us was passion or desperation or foolishness or dues from the past—but it was not love.

I reached down beside the bed and pulled out the small manila envelope in my bag, taken from Retro's files. Inside the envelope were small reproductions of the seventeen snapshot placards— photos and words—which hung in the Retro meeting room.

Casually, one by one, I laid them out on the quilt that covered us.

"What are you doing? Who are these people?"

"Dead, Tony. All of them dead. All of them died. All of them murdered by a madman who left a toy mouse for each victim's cat."

Tony stared at me, incredulous. Then he picked one photo up ... then another.

"I need your help very badly," I pleaded.

And then I told him all that had transpired. He listened carefully. We had both become so chaste, lying naked in that hotel bed. So chaste.

When I had finished my story, I added, "I know you're in the middle of bad times now Tony, but—"

He interrupted almost savagely, "Tell me what you want me to do."

"I have a list of all relatives and friends of the victims who were interviewed by the police. I want you to contact them and get them to tell you something they didn't tell the police. I have to know more from them, Tony ... little things or big things. Do you understand?"

"What are you going to do?"

"Start at the beginning . . . or the end. Go back to the scene of the last murders—the Tyre brothers."

He sat up quickly, looking for a cigarette. He could find none. He turned to me and I saw fear as well as love on his face. "I don't know what happened to us, Swede, or why it happened, but I'm very glad. Do you know what I mean? It's like we had both started classes at the Dramatic Workshop again—and the future was open . . . with all kinds of possibilities. Remember beauty and truth and authenticity and all that nonsense, Swede? Do you know what I'm saying?"

I gathered all the small photos into a pile. Yes, I knew exactly what he was saying. And I knew he would help. As to what really happened between us—in bed—well, that was a mystery.

# 8

"How long is this going to take?" Arcenaux asked nastily.

His tone took me out of a sort of tidal pool of reverie. I was wondering how close to the truth my theories were: the notion that the missing cats were the only real correlation other than the mouse toy; and my belief that the FBI agent's statistics were significant only in that they matched, in season and time, cat fertility and reproduction. Maybe the cats were not really missing ... maybe they were with relatives. And maybe the agent's findings were just statistical flukes. An air of unreality hung over all of my theories. There were too many dead people.

And I was wondering about Tony Basillio. It had been a long time since I had acted with sexual abandon.

When I didn't answer because of my reveries, Arcenaux shouted, "How many times are you going to want to come back to this apartment? I told you we went over it with a fine-tooth comb."

"This won't take long," I replied.

The dead brothers' studio apartment was as dramatic on a cloudy morning as it had been on that sunny afternoon when I first saw it. I was in a space capsule ... the glass sides of the capsule groaning in the high-swirling breezes.

I sat on a chair and stared around. The apartment emitted an almost overwhelming sense of emptiness.

"Are you sure nothing was taken from the apartment?" I asked.

"Nothing but the bodies. And the toy mouse."

"Where are their books and magazines?"

"They obviously didn't read."

"What about clothes?"

"In the hall closet, next to the bathrooms," Arcenaux said impatiently.

I walked to the closets and opened them. One contained a few suits, shirts, coats, sweaters, shoes. The other contained carefully folded linens and towels. At the bottom of the linen closet were two folded blankets. The brothers obviously slept on the sofas, not even opening them, just covering them with a blanket.

I closed the closet door and walked slowly about the large studio apartment. I realized that if I was a spectator watching a play in which the apartment was a set, I would have an overwhelming sense of abandonment—as if no one really had lived there ... or as if whoever lived there was about to move.

I stared out one line of windows. There was another, more chilling explanation of the apartment's bareness: the occupants knew they were going to die—they had made peace with the grasping world of objects by relinquishing them.

"Doesn't it strike you as odd that the apartment is so empty?" I asked Arcenaux.

"Some people like junk and some people don't," he replied.

I kept circumnavigating the apartment. There was no bric a brac at all. No ashtrays. No framed photos. No vases. No seashells. No candles or candlesticks. No things.

"Did you find out any more about the Siamese cat of theirs?"

My question embarrassed Arcenaux. "No! Not a damn thing. I mean, the doorman of this building was the one who told us a relative had taken the cat. But now he says he don't remember telling us that. And we can't find the damn relative or the damn cat."

Yes, I had expected that. I stared at the Van Gogh print on the wall . . . the one I had straightened on my first visit to the apartment.

"Which of the brothers owned the cat before they moved in together?"

"Jack."

I nodded. My concentration should be on him . . . on Jack. But both brothers remained ciphers without objects . . . without books . . . without ties to the world of things.

"Look, I'm going out for some coffee. How long will you be?" Arcenaux asked.

"Half-hour," I replied.

He slammed the door shut behind him, angrily.

I had become, I realized, a very severe thorn in Retro's side in a very swift time. But they should all cheer up—I was now only a part-time consultant.

I wandered into the walk-through kitchen. There were no cat-food bags or cans. That was strange. The refrigerator and the shelves were almost empty. A few pots and pans in the sink rack. Nothing at all on the range top.

I opened the drawers. A few sets of utensils. A can opener. I opened the cabinet over the sink. Paper plates. Paper cups. Paper towels.

Then I walked to the edge of the kitchen space and opened the broom closet. No mops. No brooms. No cleaning fluids.

In fact the broom closet was empty except for a few hanging dust rags, and on the bottom was a careful pile of dinner plates.

They were very old chipped plates, with large faded tulip designs.

I smiled sadly. At last, the first sign of the brothers' normalcy . . . of sentimentality.

Had these plates belonged to their mother? They were certainly old enough.

I bent down and plucked the first one—carefully—off the pile.

Then I stepped back startled!

Between the plate I had lifted and the second plate in the pile was a leaf.

I picked it up. No, it wasn't a single leaf. There were three leaves, one on top of each other, fastened at the stems with a large red twistum.

It was very strange. I mean, I knew of the old romantic thing of pressing leaves between the covers of a book. But between plates? I picked up the second plate. There was another bunch of leaves. And another! Between each plate were similar pressed leaves.

Bizarre! Did Jack Tyre collect leaves? But he was a white-collar worker in the Department of Parks. He worked in an office in the old Armory. Even if he collected leaves, why would he bind them and press them?

I put the plates back, took one of the leaf bunches, and went back to my chair. I sat down and turned it in my hand. It was like all the others. On top, a ginkgo leaf. Then an oak leaf. And finally, what probably was a maple leaf. And all fastened with that bold red twistum.

I sat and twirled the leaves in my hand. I held them up to the morning light. They were beautiful! They made a beautiful bouquet. The red twistum was like a valentine.

I grinned, realizing finally what I was looking at. A valentine. A love letter. Someone had sent the leaves to Jack Tyre. They were indeed love letters and that was why he had pressed them between his mother's old plates.

But so what? What did it mean? Neither the murderer nor the police had found them, or, if they had, had paid any attention to the leaves. What did a strange, somewhat imaginative bouquet of leaves have to do with a toy mouse, a

missing Siamese cat, and all those other murders?

I heard the door open. "You ready? You finished?" Arcenaux barked out.

I slipped the leaf bouquet into my bag. It was
better to follow up on these leaves, however absurd they were, than spend hours at Retro facing
the unit's scorn for me ... for their resident cat
woman. Besides, I might find something. So
might Basillio. And the only thing the computer
was going to find was what that strange little
man Bert Turk told it to find.

"I'm ready," I said, and we left the apartment.

# 9

The phone rang as I was undressing for bed. It was early for me, only about ten P.M. But it had been a long day. Bushy was already on my pillow, exhausted after a long day sleeping on the living-room rug.

It was my agent. She said that a Japanese film company was doing a program on Western theater people's response to Kabuki. Would I be interested? There would be some remuneration. I told her no. She said brightly: "Okay. I'll be in touch." And that was that.

Eight minutes later Tony Basillio called. The sound of his voice on the other end of the line startled me. It was as if he was there to demand comments from me on what had happened on that hotel bed. What were we: lovers? No. I still couldn't sort out what had happened and what else should happen, if anything.

"I found someone, Swede, you have to meet. He wants to see you now."

"Now?"

"His name is Karl Bonaventura."

"Jill Bonaventura's husband?" I asked.

"No. Her brother."

"Bring him over," I urged, and hung up the phone. Jill Bonaventura was victim number three. Murdered nine years ago at age thirty-one. Strangled.

Twenty minutes later they were both in my living room. Tony still looked terrible. But at least his eyes were focused and he had shaved.

Karl Bonaventura was an enormous man, dressed in a very beat-up denim jumpsuit. He owned some kind of auto-repair service. The moment Tony introduced him to me, he grabbed my hand as if I was a healer.

Then he apologized for his enthusiasm. "I'm sorry. But you don't know how long I have been waiting for someone to take an interest in Jill's murder. Do you think those cops did anything? Those people like Arcenaux and the others? They did nothing. They know nothing. They forgot all about her."

He started to cry suddenly, powerfully, his body racked with sobs. Tony made a silent gesture with his hands. I nodded. I have rarely experienced such explosive grief in a person ... particularly since it was now more than nine years after the death of his sister.

"She was a beautiful young woman. No one knew how beautiful she really was. It wasn't fair for that to happen. It just wasn't fair." He was now trying to talk between sobs. "One moment she was alive. And the next moment someone had strangled the life out of her body. I couldn't let it end there. I won't let it end—ever."

Tony placed a consoling hand on Karl's shoulder and finally coaxed him down onto the sofa. I remembered the computer printouts of the interviews with Karl Bonaventura. The man had seemed as overcome with grief then as he was now—and nothing he told the police had proved of any value in the investigation.

"Mr. Bonaventura has been constantly in touch with the police over the past nine years," Tony explained to me, "but they ignore him."

"Do you know that the police now believe that the same individual who murdered your sister murdered sixteen other individuals?" I asked him.

He began to sob again and then caught himself. "I don't care about the others. For nine years I have been looking for my sister's killer. Every day that passes, I want to crawl in the grave with her. I have hired private investigators . . . I have called the FBI . . . I have done everything I could . . . and it's all nothing. But they won't stop me. I don't care how long it takes. I don't care if I have to crawl on my knees to the phone . . . I . . ." He bent over suddenly as if in great pain, then sat up and was silent, the tears streaming from his eyes.

I walked quickly into the kitchen and brought him back a small glass of cold orange juice. He took it from me—a big hand, rough from work—and held the glass against his lips without drinking. It was very painful to watch such abysmal grief, to be in the presence of a man who had simply refused to end the torment of his sister's death. It was sad and pathetic and painful, and somehow glorious.

I could see that Tony was becoming paler and paler in the face of the brother's sobbing words. And I still didn't know why he had brought the man to my apartment. Karl Bonaventura did not seem rational enough to make any contribution to the case. All he had was his horror.

Tony moved closer to me and placed his arm lightly on the back of my neck. I moved away quickly, suddenly afraid of further contact with him.

He shook his head as if to assure me that he wasn't really interested in a sexual encounter—he was trying to explain.

"Mr. Bonaventura has something," he said, "that will be of interest to you."

"What are you talking about, Tony?"

"He can take you to his sister's apartment."

I didn't understand what Tony was talking about. I stared at Karl. The large man was nodding his head vigorously.

"Tony," I said gently, "his sister died nine years ago."

"He has maintained his sister's apartment."

"What do you mean 'maintained' it?"

"He has paid rent on the apartment for the last nine years. He considers it a kind of shrine. The apartment is exactly as it was on the night his sister was murdered. Nothing has been removed. Nothing has been changed."

"Is that true, Mr. Bonaventura?" I asked.

He reached in his pocket and pulled out a color photo of his sister. He held it up for me to see. "She still lives there. In her apartment. One-Hundred and Eleventh Street and Broadway. She still lives there and I still visit her."

I couldn't look at the photo. I turned away. But this strange man had provided us with an invaluable time capsule. It was a gift that we had no right to expect; a chance to go back, far back, to one of the first murders ... to attempt to recreate the murder in its pristine state.

"I'll call you, Tony. We'll set it up with Mr. Bonaventura, if he doesn't mind taking us there."

"He wants very much to take us there," Tony said.

Tony then helped the big man up and they walked to the door. I opened it for them.

"Can you wait outside in the hall for a minute?" Tony asked Bonaventura. He closed the door partway after the man exited.

"We have to think about what happened the other day, Swede," he whispered to me.

Before I could respond, he kissed me quickly on the lips. He tasted of whiskey.

"I think we made a mistake, Tony," I replied.

He tried to kiss me again but I turned my face away. He whispered into my ear, " 'If this be error and upon me proved ... I never writ nor no man ever loved.' "

"I thought you loathed Shakespeare, Tony."

"That was in another life. I am brand-new. Everything is new again."

He walked out the door. I shut it. Turning, I saw that Bushy was sitting in the hallway, regarding me quizzically. I realized that I hadn't even told Tony about the leaf valentines I had found pressed between plates in Jack Tyre's apartment. My negligence irritated me.

"What are you staring at?" I yelled at Bushy. I think he grinned.

# 10

When I awoke the next morning, Pancho was lying on the end of my bed. His eyes were open and he seemed to be staring at Bushy, who was stretched out, as usual, on the pillow next to me.

This was very strange. Pancho never slept on my bed ... if he ever slept at all. Was he sick? Had he finally escaped from his imaginary pursuers? Was he about to attack Bushy? Or me?

I lay in bed and stared at my dear crazy cat. The other one, sober Bushy, was still snoozing against the pillow. As I looked at Pancho I realized that he was my feline analogue for Tony Basillio. Pancho was Tony. Tony was Pancho. That was why it had happened. Like sometimes my heart overflowed for Pancho's plight—so it had overflowed for Tony Basillio in the hotel room. It was love, yes, but not the normal kind. I had slept with him, I realized, to protect him. Against what? Who knows? As many things as were chasing Pancho—so they were chasing Tony.

I moved my toes just a bit, and Pancho flew away, leaving only the slight indentation of his body on the quilt.

An hour later, having forgotten all about my strange analogy between Pancho and Tony, I entered my new cubicle at Retro. It was pathetic. A tiny Plexiglas square set down by the supply room.

It was, I realized, designed as punishment. Or rather, Judy Mizener had put me in it to show the other people in Retro that I could no longer be taken seriously, although I was still part of the team.

When I entered the computer room, Bert Turk was polite and distant; no more marriage proposals. He handed me the updated blue book. I went over the files on Jill Bonaventura's brother—nothing new. And then I carefully studied all the information and profiles on Jack Tyre. There was no mention of leaves of any kind. With Bert Turk's help, I then did a computer search for any mention of leaf bouquets in any one of the other murders. There was no mention at all— not a single reference. It was time to go to Tyre's workplace.

Twenty minutes later I took a cab up to the main Department of Parks administration building, which stands just inside the Fifth Avenue entrance of the Zoo. I found Frank Ardmore on the second floor of the building in a small office. He was not happy to see me.

"I don't understand. Are you a cop?"

"No. I'm just temporarily attached to a special unit that is investigating Jack Tyre's murder— and his brother's."

"Well, I spoke to the cops for hours. I told them everything I knew. Which wasn't much. Look, the man worked right next door to me for a long time. We were friendly. We talked together all the time. But not after work. He went his way and I went mine."

"Did you ever see these?" I asked.

Frank Ardmore stared down at the small leaf bouquet I held in my hand.

"What the hell is that?" he asked. He kept on adjusting his stubby tie. He had a whole raft of pencils and pens in his shirt pocket, which seemed about ready to fall out.

"Three leaves tied together with a twistum." I opened the red twistum and laid the three leaves on my arm.

He shook his head in confusion.

"Did Jack Tyre collect leaves?"

"Are you kidding? I don't know what you mean. Collect leaves? Thousands of tons of leaves are collected in this park in the fall. Jack didn't work in that department. Did he like trees? How the hell should I know? Could he identify trees? Probably. Most people who work in parks with a lot of trees can identify them. Even I can do that."

He leaned over and pointed. "That is a ginkgo leaf. That is an oak leaf. And that ..." He paused. He picked up the third leaf. "And that looks like a leaf from a Chinese maple on the Seventy-second Street footpath, which by the way, is one of the oldest living trees in the park."

I rebound the leaves. He was not a friendly man. Not at all.

I stared at him. There was something strange about his discomfort in my questions.

"Is there anything about Jack Tyre that you forgot to tell the police?"

"Like what?"

"You tell me."

"Yeah. He didn't like Chinese food," Frank Ardmore replied sarcastically.

"Thank you for your help," I replied, equally sarcastically, and started to walk away.

"Wait a minute. If you want to find out about leaves, why don't you see Georgina Kulaks. She's in charge of tree maintenance around here."

"Where do I find her?"

"I think they're working on that European beech near the bow bridge, on the south end of the lake."

I walked out of the administration building and headed uptown and west through the park. At Bethesda Fountain I cut into one of the footpaths and headed toward the lake. It was a beautiful day. People were walking arm in arm. There were dogs and baby carriages and kite fliers.

As I walked down the grassy knoll to the bow bridge I saw a small team of workers near a massive low-crowned tree. That must be the European beech. When I got closer I realized they were all men. Then I caught sight of a woman standing about twenty yards away from the group, closer to the lake. She was holding a clipboard and staring out across the lake.

I walked up to her. She nodded in a friendly fashion.

"Are you Georgina Kulaks?" I asked.

She nodded and waited, smiling. She was a short, slight woman with brown hair pulled back. She was wearing regulation parks-department pants and a sweatshirt. Her face was lined.

"My name is Alice Nestleton. I'd like to ask you a few questions about Jack Tyre."

Her eyes opened wide in horror. They stared down at my hand. I realized I was holding the bunch of leaves in plain view.

Her face seemed to crumble ... to dissolve. She turned away from me quickly and knelt down. The sobs seemed to explode from her body.

It had all happened so quickly ... I was so startled ... I didn't know what to do.

Then I knelt beside her and tried to comfort her as best I could. It was obvious I had found Jack Tyre's lover, the woman who had sent him the strange valentines.

Slowly she began to regain control of herself. Her fingers held the clipboard so tightly the blood drained from her hands and wrists and became chalk white.

"Please. You have to tell me what you know about Jack Tyre. The same madman who killed him murdered more than a dozen other people. Tell me what you know about him."

She nodded vigorously. She started to breathe

deeply in and out. She was coming around. I helped her up. She placed her arm in mine for support and we slowly started to walk along the edge of the lake.

"It was just seeing those leaves again," she said, "and thinking of that wonderful man. It was so terrible. We were lovers for three years. He broke if off about a year ago. I couldn't understand why. We were very happy together. And I sort of became childish and kept sending him those leaves. I never believed he would keep them. And he must have kept them ... or how would you have found them."

"He kept them. He treasured them," I affirmed.

She stopped and stared out over the water.

"He was such a wonderful man. So strange and gentle and wise. Do you see those trees on the other side of the lake? That's the Ramble, one of the most isolated parts of the park. He used to go there on the weekends, with his cat on his shoulder, and wander around there. He told me he had found some of the old caves near the water and his cat used to love to prowl around there.

"And on lunch hours he used to go to the Metropolitan Museum. To the Egyptian Wing. How he loved that place. People loved him. He was sort of an informal tour guide. He knew everything. I can't explain what a gentle man he was. I had never met anyone like him. Do you know where we made love all the time? In all kinds of weather? There, across the lake, in the Ramble.

At first I thought he just didn't want me to come to his apartment. But no, it wasn't that. He wanted to make love in the park—that's all."

The tears came again. She leaned her cheek against the clipboard. Then she continued.

"And then, suddenly, he told me he couldn't see me anymore, that he was going on some kind of trip. And he just broke it off. He wouldn't even say hello when we passed each other in the park. I didn't know what to do, so I started sending him those leaves . . . like a stupid little girl."

"Did you speak to the police?"

"No. No one ever knew we were lovers. No one."

"What kind of trip was he talking about?"

"I couldn't find out. It was all so strange and terrible. Look, I have to go now. I have to go."

But she didn't go. She started to tap one hand against her clipboard. It made the strangest noise.

"Who are you?" she asked suddenly, as if ashamed of having revealed so much to a total stranger who had not really identified herself. Or worse, as if she had been fooled into one of those brief friendships which are totally delusional.

"I'm a consultant with a major-crimes unit of the New York Police Department. My responsibilities include investigating the murder of the Tyre brothers. I am, however, not interviewing you in any official capacity."

"What does that mean?" she asked.

I shrugged. I didn't answer. I felt stupid. I don't know why I said that.

She was looking at me now ... evaluating.

Perhaps in the same way she evaluated trees before her crew worked on them—with pruning shears, wires, pesticides.

I knew I should keep my mouth shut. I knew she was making some kind of decision.

"He had a secret life," she said quietly.

Her statement confused me.

"In what sense secret?"

"In the sense that he kept it from me, that he hid it, that there was something else he was about ... Do you know what I mean?"

"Drugs? Alcohol? Gambling? Do you mean something like that?"

"Oh, no, not that," she said quickly.

I waited for her to speak again. She seemed to be struggling to articulate something.

"I felt," she finally said in a very measured tone, "that we had become so close, Jack and I, that I was impinging on that secret ... and that he had to dispense with me."

"Did he ever say that?" I asked.

"Say what?"

"Did he use the word 'dispense' with you?"

"No."

"But you felt that."

"What other thing could it be? Why would he suddenly just break it off?"

"Then you didn't believe what he said about a trip?"

"No."

For the first time since we had been moving

along the shore of the lake, I saw rowboats on the water. They came into view from under the bow bridge. There were four of them. Two had children wearing orange life preservers. It dawned on me that I had no idea whatsoever how deep the Central Park Lake was. Was it shallow or a hundred feet deep?"

"I know," Georgina Kulaks said, "that you're thinking I'm just a rejected lover ..."

She paused and laughed bitterly, then continued: "And that this secret life of Jack's is all in my head, an attempt to excuse or explain the inexplicable in a favorable light—just why he broke off the affair. I know that's what you're thinking. But believe me, I'm not a fool. And I'm not a girl anymore."

We stopped our slow walk and turned our backs to the lake. I could see her looking at the men who were pruning the European beech.

"Was his brother somehow connected to Jack's secret life?"

"I don't think so. For some reason, Jack always kept me away from his brother."

"Why?"

"I don't know. It didn't matter anyway."

"Do you think that this secret life you're talking about ... this intuitive feeling you have that such a life existed ... do you think that this was the cause of his murder?"

"I don't know."

"Were you aware ... or rather did you have this feeling that he had a secret life before the breakup? I mean, after all, he obviously tried to keep you out of his apartment and away from his brother."

The anger flared in her eyes.

"Are you saying that he wanted to make love to me in the park, like homeless people, because he didn't want to take me to his apartment?"

She was very defensive now. Precarious. Irrational. I could see that clearly. I could see her fighting to keep her mental balance.

"I'm sorry I snapped at you," she said. "Forget what I told you. Forget everything! It doesn't mean anything now—at all. He's dead. He's gone."

She looked for a moment like she was going to collapse. She grasped the clipboard until her knuckles were white. She steadied herself.

"What I'm trying to tell you is that he was different."

Her voice was cracking. But it was an angry voice.

"Don't you understand me?"

She started to point at me . . . her finger punching the air as if to accentuate her words.

"Jack Tyre was different."

She started to sob. She caught herself. She gasped for enough breath to tell me more.

"He was a beautiful man!"

This time her voice came out so loud that I could see some of her men near the tree turn toward the sound. Her voice was becoming louder and louder and more excited.

"He gave me the three best years of my life and I don't understand any of it now ... any of it ... except that he's dead and I couldn't see him or talk to him or touch him before he died."

She walked away from me quickly.

"Wait," I called out to her as she started to walk away. I held out the leaf bouquet, now bedraggled. "Take it."

She shook her head violently and kept walking. I turned back toward the lake. I realized that from now on I would have to input into the Retro data base all that I found. Everything. Too much stuff was surfacing to keep in my head. Besides, like it or not, I was part of a team. An ensemble. The Retro Drama Workshop. I laughed to myself. No, The Judy Mizener Players.

My eyes wandered to the thick growth in the Ramble. I could visualize Jack Tyre, his cat draped around his shoulders, wandering there. But my vision of Tyre was fuzzy. His lover's description of him did not really tally with the profile in Retro. Georgina Kulaks had called him strange and kind and wise. It was almost as if she was describing a wonder worker or a healer or a holy man. I closed my eyes. It was easy to think of the Siamese being taken for his weekend play into the Ramble—purring and chatting as he let himself be transported. I could see the ears and the magnificently formed face. And the eyes—the bold fey eyes, large ... too large for

71

the exquisite body. Where was that lovely cat now? I knew then, for the first time, that the murders were about something else . . . about life and death . . . about grace.

# 11

Tony and I sat in a coffee shop on 110th and Broadway. We were a bit early to meet Karl Bonaventura, who was going to take us to his sister's bizarrely preserved apartment.

Tony was not impressed by my interview with Jack Tyre's lover. "So what did you learn? That they made love in the park? That Jack was a bit weird?"

"What I learned, Tony, is that something is very wrong ... odd ... strange."

He laughed. "Oh, come on, Swede. It was all wrong before you met this Georgina. I mean, toy mice and vanished cats and every victim dying in a different way, and time sequences between murders that mimic cat-gestation periods."

"Then you don't think there was one killer?"

"I really have no idea. What do I know?" He looked at me slyly and then added: "After all, I'm just an out-of-work scenic designer."

"How *is* your new life coming?" I asked.

He reached across the small table, grabbed my hand, and kissed it. I pulled my hand back. His face was all lit up.

"It's going to work," he said. "I moved into the

Wellington on Fifty-fifth Street and Seventh, a monthly rate. My wife has calmed down. The stores are running themselves. And my kids— well, who knows? The fact of the matter is ..."

He stopped in mid-sentence. I waited. He remained silent.

"The fact of the matter is what, Tony?" I asked.

His face clouded over. "The fact of the matter, Swede, is that you don't even remember this place."

"What place?"

"This coffee shop."

"Should I?" I didn't know what he was talking about.

"Yes, you should. Because the floor above this coffee shop used to be a cabaret. Me and you used to go here. In the seventies. Don't you remember? Eric Bentley started it ... as a place for political theater. Guerrilla theater coming off the street and into the loft and made even wilder and more pungent."

I leaned back. I remembered now. Oh, how long ago it had been! How very long. It always seemed to be raining when we attended a performance, and there was always the smell of damp clothes.

"That time, Tony, is dead and gone," I finally said.

"Yes, with O'Leary in the grave."

"And it is not coming back, Tony. There will be no Brecht revival in our lifetime, Tony. There will be no theater of the absurd. There is nothing around for us to do. Don't you understand that, Tony? LaMaMa doesn't exist anymore as we knew it. The Wooster Group is gone. *Dionysus '69* is a memory. That's why your move to dump everything and return to the theater disturbs me. Tony, there are no parts for me anymore because there is no audience. And it's going to be the same for you."

"Oh, ye of little faith," he replied, stirring his coffee reflectively.

The large, pained face of Karl Bonaventura suddenly loomed in the window behind Tony.

We quickly left the coffee shop and together with Karl walked to his sister's apartment. It was in one of those large old apartment buildings which fronted Broadway but which had the entrance on the side street.

The moment I walked in, I realized that Karl had told the truth, as sad as it was. Nothing seemed to have been touched in nine years. It appeared that even the clothes Jill had dropped on a chair before her murder had been left. The apartment looked as if its tenant could return at any time and continue her existence.

I sat down quickly. The realization that I had entered a shrine of Karl Bonaventura's making made me weak.

The apartment was small. A living room. One small bedroom. Kitchen and bathroom. It had obviously once been part of a very large floor-through apartment and then divided and subdivided as many of the old West Side buildings had been.

"Nothing has been touched except to clean," Karl said, and his face registered a little bit of shame, a little bit of defiance, and a great deal of grief. I looked quickly at Tony, who also seemed overcome by the shrine.

"Only these are new," Karl said, pointing to a vase full of freshly cut carnations—red and white—on the small coffee table.

"I bring her flowers from time to time," he said.

Tony stared at me. We both had the same thought. This large man with us was possibly deranged. That kind of grief and denial could not last nine years with such intensity.

I let my eyes wander about. Jill had liked bright bold colors. The furniture was all obviously secondhand—the computer had told me she was unemployed at the time of her death—but had been recovered with bright fabrics. The lamp shades were particularly raucous in color—a few of them even striped blues, whites, reds, oranges.

"How did she support herself?" I asked.

"She's a songwriter," her brother said. "She has a hard time. She can't get a break. She does all kinds of odd jobs—waitress, typist, you know."

It was very disconcerting to hear him use the present tense—as if she was still alive.

"What kind of songs?"

"Not that rock-and-roll garbage," he declared, wringing his large powerful hands together.

"Beautiful stuff—folk songs. I think you would call them folk songs."

"Did you help her out financially?"

"She doesn't want my help. I keep offering, but she refuses. Only once a year would she take anything."

"Why once a year? You mean at Christmas?" I pressed.

"No. It was funny. Once a year she needed twenty-five hundred dollars."

"For what?"

"She never said. She just needed it. And she wanted it a certain way. She wanted twenty-five hundred-dollar bills."

"Didn't you think that strange?" Tony asked.

"Sure. It was strange. But she wanted it and I gave it to her. I would have given her a helluva lot more."

"So you gave it to her every year?"

"Well. The year she was murdered. And the year before that. And the year before that. I think three years in all."

What an odd development. I didn't know what to make of it.

So I changed the subject. "Tell me about her cat."

"Oh, Missy. I really didn't like that cat. She was crazy. A big old white cat with longish hair. Jill told me she was one-fifth Persian. But Jill loved her very much. Hell, she used to write notes to her."

"Write notes?"

"Yes. I'm not lying. When you get a chance, go into the kitchen. All her unpaid grocery and cleaning bills are still tacked on the bulletin board. Turn them over. You'll see. She used to leave notes near Missy's food dish. She'd ask Missy how she liked her new songs. As if Missy could read."

"What happened to Missy?"

He stood up suddenly and stared around the room as if he had heard something . . . as if in his deranged mind his sister was approaching or leaving.

"I don't know what happened to the cat," he said. "My sister had a neighbor who held an extra set of keys to her apartment. After Jill was murdered a neighborhood kid showed up and said that Jill had told him to take care of the cat if anything happened to her. The neighbor let the kid in. And he took the cat. Well, at least Missy got a good home."

"Who was the kid?" Tony asked.

"We never found out. A kid. Just a kid. From the neighborhood."

Karl Bonaventura sat down again. Then he stood up again. He seemed to be getting more and more agitated by our questions.

"Do you want to look around?" he asked. I nodded but did not move. He stood up again. "Well, take your time. Look all you want. I have to get back to work. Just shut the door when you leave; it locks automatically." He left the apartment, slamming the door behind him.

"He frightens me and I don't trust him," I said to Tony.

"He frightens me also," Tony admitted.

I closed my eyes. The apartment was oppressive. It was not the kind of shrine or memorial that one could deal with rationally. Jill Bonaventura seemed to hover about every piece of furniture.

"We won't learn anything here, Swede," I heard Tony say.

"I think you're wrong. I think we'll learn everything here."

"That man is crazy, Swede. He really believes his sister is alive when he comes in here. He's hypnotized with grief over her memory, yet he really doesn't admit she's dead. Swede, you can't take anything he says seriously."

"I took very seriously what he said about Jill's cat. And about the twenty-five hundred dollars he gave her for three years prior to her death."

"Do you think a neighborhood kid stole the cat? And if he did . . . so what? Maybe he thought he could sell it."

"Tony, listen, I don't know what any of what he told us means . . . but I feel that I'm in the center of things . . . do you understand? Just sitting here . . . don't you feel it?"

"You're getting very weird, Swede. What are you trying to tell me? That being here in this apartment is sending you into some mystical realm? Are you becoming a psychic, Swede? Don't we have enough trouble?"

I opened my eyes and looked around at the many multicolored lamp shades. I did feel something very weird. A sense that I was grappling with the entire evil ... a sense perhaps that both Karl Bonaventura and Georgina Kulaks would kill, could kill—perhaps had killed.

It was as if all seventeen of the victims over the years were wired into that vase of carnations. It was as if they were watching me perform and they had the correct script ... only they. I became more and more uncomfortable.

"Let's look over the bedroom," I said to Tony.

We walked into the small room, dominated by a low double bed. There was a floor lamp, a chest, one bookcase, and a small dressing table with a mirror.

On the wall were three Japanese prints. Each one featured an ox. I had seen them before ... they were prints associated with Zen Buddhism. The ox was the mind that had to be tamed and refined and brought to enlightenment.

Something else was familiar ... something else I had seen before.

I sat down suddenly on the bed. All of the pictures were crooked.

"What's the matter, Swede? You look like you've seen a ghost."

"Those pictures are crooked," I replied.

"So what?"

"The Van Gogh print in Jack Tyre's apartment was also crooked."

"A lot of pictures on a lot of walls are crooked, Swede. That's the way of the world."

I ignored his comment. "Tony, do you remember that Mother Goose Rhyme, 'There Was a Crooked Man'?"

"I wasn't a big reader, Swede."

I recited it for him:

There was a crooked man,
    And he went a crooked mile,
He found a crooked sixpence
    Against a crooked stile;
He bought a crooked cat,
    Which caught a crooked mouse,
And they all lived together
    In a little crooked house.

Tony stared at me. Then he quickly straightened the pictures and sat down on the bed beside me.

"That takes care of that, Swede."

"It takes care of nothing, Tony. Don't you see?"

"See what?"

"All these tiny little crazy things ... toy mice and crooked pictures and leaf bouquets and cats who vanish with nonexistent relatives and dingy apartments maintained as shrines. Don't you see?"

"See what?" he repeated.

I couldn't answer him. I lay back on the bed. Seventeen beautiful people had died in pain and terror. For what?

81

Tony lay down beside me. The moment he put his hand on my face I knew we were going to make love again, right there, on Jill Bonaventura's bed.

We lay in the bed afterward for a long time. Neither of us spoke. The afternoon shadows were beginning to envelop us. From time to time I heard sounds, as if Jill's cat Missy was prowling about—her large white cat whom she had loved dearly.

Finally Tony said, "Let's get out of here."

"Not yet, Tony, not yet. I want to look at those bills in the kitchen. The ones her brother told us about. The ones on which she wrote her notes to her cat."

Tony groaned. "Even you, Swede, don't write notes to your cats."

"How do you know that?"

He didn't answer. We dressed quickly. Again I had that feeling that although we had made love, Tony was not my lover. Age? Was it age? Was I beginning finally to view sex as a function? As a necessary script? My God!

The bills were thumbtacked to a small bulletin board in the kitchen. They were nine years old. Bills from druggists and bodegas and cleaning establishments.

"I wonder if her brother paid them," Tony said.

I spread the soiled bills out on the small table. On the back of each one was a sad silly note to her cat. "Dear Missy" each one started out. And then: "I hope you like your food. What do you think of these lyrics?" And then there was a stanza or two of a song she was writing—usually about love and mountain streams ... or husbands dying in the war. Often mawkish. Often cliché. But sometimes lovely.

It was easy to imagine her writing the notes and then slipping them under the cat's food bowl. Yes, it was so easy to imagine it. Foolish. Charming. The kind of inexplicable behavior that cats seem to elicit in their glorious way. They make their humans into lovable fools.

The last bill was dated only two days before her death. It was from a pharmacy and I couldn't read the druggist's writing. The bill totaled $11.60.

I turned it over. It was a different kind of note. It read: "Dear Missy. Your trip to the Desolate Swamp will be gentle. I promise you. You'll ride in the front. No crate for you. And you'll have all the hacked chicken you want. Without sesame sauce."

I pushed the note away from me, toward the center of the table. Tony took it and read it. "What the hell was she talking about? These aren't song lyrics."

"It was probably the last thing she wrote on earth, Tony. The very last thing." We both stared at the small piece of soiled paper.

"Well," Tony said, "I know what hacked chicken is. A Chinese dish. I used to eat it all the time. But I liked it with the sesame sauce. What cat wouldn't like cold sliced chicken?"

I read the note again. Missy was going on a journey. A long journey, or there wouldn't have been mention of a crate. And she was going in a car or a truck. And Jill had promised Missy that she would be riding in the front seat next to the driver. I told my thoughts to Tony. He agreed at first. But then he said: "No. Wrong. The whole thing is some kind of fantasy."

"Why fantasy?" I asked.

"Desolate Swamp. There's no such place except in the imagination. It's a romantic metaphor for something."

"You mean like the veterinarian?"

"That's stretching it a bit."

"Then what?"

"I don't know. I did hear of a place called the Great Dismal Swamp. I think it's in Georgia."

I kept picking up the paper and putting it down. Was it possible that the neighborhood boy who had taken Missy was the one who had taken her on this journey to the Desolate Swamp? Yes. This was no romantic metaphor. Jill Bonaventura had given me something concrete—across time and space.

"Tony, I think there is a real place called Desolate Swamp."

"In the land of Oz."

"No, a real place. We're going to have to find it."

"How?"

"Topographical maps. Atlases. I don't know, Tony. That'll be your job."

"Swede, this is a long shot. A very pathetic long shot. We're grasping at straws. We're starting to look stupid." I silenced him by putting my fingers on his lips.

# 12

"So, Abelard, if you can hear me—and I am sure you can hear me, even under the furniture— answer me these questions. Why did her brother give Jill Bonaventura twenty-five hundred dollars each year? Why did Georgina Kulaks send Jack Tyre a leaf bouquet? Why did that neighborhood kid take Missy after Jill Bonaventura was murdered? Why did Jack Tyre take his cat into the park every weekend? Why did the murderer leave a toy mouse for each cat?"

I shut up, then cocked my ear and waited. I knew Abelard was hiding under the large mahogany desk I was seated at. I heard him. Of course, I had given up all hope of ever seeing him. But I could communicate with him other than by cat-sitting chores.

No answer. I tapped the top of the desk to get his attention. "And why did the murderer make the pictures crooked?" It was hopeless. Abelard would not help me.

I stared at one of Mrs. Salzman's many wall clocks. It was 11:20 in the morning. Tony was at the large library on Forty-second Street trying to find something ... anything ... about a place called Desolate Swamp, which may not have been a place at all, but may have been some romantic knot in Jill Bonaventura's heart.

Tony had all three numbers—my apartment, Retro, and Mrs. Salzman. The moment he found something, he would call.

I left the sitting room, where I had been conversing with the submerged Abelard—if indeed he was in that room at all—and went into the kitchen to start preparing his food. I really couldn't remember when I had fed him last because I kept altering the times I visited him. Poor Abelard ... he was saddled with an erratic cat sitter.

The moment I entered the kitchen, I saw the note pinned, or rather Scotch-taped, to the refrigerator door.

My heart sank. Had Mrs. Salzman terminated my services? Had she found out I was visiting poor Abelard in an erratic pattern?

No! It was not a termination notice. On the contrary, she asked if I could cat sit for Abelard a few more times. YES, I wrote in large letters with a red Magic Marker on the bottom of the note. God bless you, Mrs. Salzman, wherever you are, and whomever.

I opened the refrigerator door and laughed out loud.

Inside, on the second shelf, were nine tiny pink mice, all lined up.

Each one had a chocolate nose.

Each one had a chocolate tail.

Each one had chocolate ears.

Who were they for? Me? Or Abelard? I picked one up and sniffed it. Marzipan. Nine little marzipan mice. I closed the door. Maybe tomorrow I would consume them. Let them rest now. I listened for some sound of movement. None. It came to me . . . the idea . . . that I should one day bring Bushy and Pancho to Mrs. Salzman's apartment. Maybe they could flush out Abelard. If not they, who?

I was so lost in the possibilities surrounding this fantasy that I didn't hear the phone until it had rung three times. Then I picked it up. It was Tony and he was so excited I could barely understand him. He told me to meet him in a bar on Madison between Fortieth and Thirty-ninth Street. It had an Irish name—something like Emerald Rock. In an hour.

The bar was ghastly—crowded, noisy, stuffy. I spotted him at one of the tables eating a hot turkey sandwich with a knife and fork. In front of him was an enormous glass of what seemed to be ale.

"Swede," he called out. I slipped into the chair across the table from him and stared at the sandwich.

"Do you want one?" he asked, smiling broadly. He was obviously enjoying it.

"What did you learn in the library?"

Carefully, almost ceremoniously, he laid his

knife and fork down, took a sip of the ale, then wiped his mouth with a paper napkin.

"Fascinating stuff, Swede," he said.

"What do you mean, fascinating?"

He lowered his voice. "Did you ever hear of the Goddess Astarte?"

"No."

"A goddess in ancient Babylonia. A kind of ferocious lady who would drink blood on occasion. But she also had her kindly side. And according to ancient myth, once a year she journeyed into the bowels of the earth to bring back a god of fertility who was being imprisoned there. The moment he was safe on the surface of the earth, the flowers began to bloom and, poof—there was spring."

"A very nice myth, Tony, but what does this have to do with Jill Bonaventura's note to her cat, Missy?"

"Well, Swede, according to the ancient Babylonian texts, the place where the God of Spring was always imprisoned in the underworld was called Desolate Swamp."

I didn't know how to reply. I was dumbfounded. I didn't know what I had expected, but I hadn't expected this. I stared at Tony.

Suddenly the sides of his face began to quiver, and a moment later he burst into laughter. "You believed me ... you believed it ..." he kept repeating, laughing until the tears rolled down his cheeks.

There was nothing I could do but sit there and wait until he laughed himself out at my expense.

"I'm sorry, Swede," he said after he had finally collected himself.

"Forget it, Tony, it's just that sometimes your perpetually arrested adolescence is tedious."

"Well, you won't find this tedious," he replied, slapping a road map onto the table.

I picked the map up. It read: "Full-Color Interstate 87 Map—New York to Montreal—Montreal to New York."

"What is Eighty-seven?" I asked.

"The New York Thruway." He opened the map and spread it out.

His finger started moving north on 87. "Here we go, Swede, going north. We reach Albany in a couple of hours. That's halfway to Canada. We keep going. See, there's Lake George. Now we go a little further. Schroon Lake. You see it? Fine. Now, just get off the highway and go about ten miles east. What do you see?"

The letters were small and blurred and hard to read. I squinted. They began to make sense. I put the letters together: "DESOLATE SWAMP."

"My God, Tony, it's right on the map. It exists as a real place."

"Right. That's the Adirondacks, Swede, that's a long way up."

I studied the words again. There seemed to be a lot of ponds and small streams in the area. Next to Desolate Swamp was something called Glidden Swamp.

I sat back in the chair and smiled at Tony. It was the first real break we had made in the case. Or rather, it was the first destination we could see.

"You have to go up there, Tony."

His face dropped. "Swede, this map is all very nice, but Jill Bonaventura wrote that note nine years ago. Her cat is long dead. So what am I going up there for?"

"I don't know."

"Then why go up?"

"It seems to me to be the intelligent thing to do."

"Intelligent? Fine! But what do I look for?"

"Anything."

"I don't have a car, Swede. I left it with my wife."

"Then rent one."

He grimaced. Then he picked up his knife and fork and proceeded to finish his sandwich, staring at me from time to time. When the entire plate was finished, he pushed it away and said, "I'll go up there, Swede, but believe me, I'm beginning to feel like a crooked picture on the wall."

"Welcome back to the theater, love."

# 13

My tiny Retro cubicle had become crowded. I sat there grimacing at a thick sheaf of photos that I had somehow found room for. They were crime-scene photos, almost all the ones the computer could cough up after arguing with that madman Bert the Turk ... I mean, Bert Turk. He didn't want to give me anything. It was hard to believe that the first time he saw me he had proposed marriage.

All the excitement had faded. I had asked for the photos to see if there were other crooked pictures ... if the pictures hung in the other victims' apartments were crooked like the ones I had found in the Tyre and Bonaventura apartments. Mother Goose was very powerful. I did not play around with Mother Goose. The crooked man with the crooked cat could well have been in the mind of the madman who murdered seventeen people.

The joke, alas, was on me. The crime-scene photos, which had been taken over the years, did not cover the walls—just the victims. All I had on the desk were grisly photos of the bodies when they were found. No walls. No pictures. I recited the Mother Goose rhyme over to myself silently. It was logical to follow that up, but the threads were now lost.

"Did you find what you were looking for?" A voice rang out from behind me. I half-turned in the cramped space. It was Judy Mizener.

"No. I didn't."

She eased herself into the cubicle and leaned against my crowded desk.

"How are the Retro meetings going? Now that I'm no longer invited, I miss them."

Mizener smiled. "The last one was pretty good. One of the detectives developed a profile."

"A profile? Of whom?"

"Of the killer."

"Based on what?"

"Well, based on the FBI data."

"But I told you his figures may have been right but his interpretation of those figures absurd."

"Yes, I know you did. I remember what you said—that they were related to physiological cycles in cats. Well, just because you say it doesn't make it right. No one else in Retro believes it either."

There was an awkward silence. She turned awkwardly to stare at the pile of crime-scene photos on my desk.

"You know," she said in an odd voice, "we're about the same age."

"I thought," I replied, "I was a little bit younger." My reply had nothing to do with looks. And I had no idea at all how old she really was.

It was a gentle rebuke at her stubbornness—an almost geriatric inability at Retro to enlarge their analysis.

"Probably," she said thoughtfully, ignoring my quip, "if we had met under some other circumstances, we would have been good friends."

"Who knows?" I replied.

"After all," she continued, smiling, "we both like the same things."

I looked at her quizzically.

"Oh, I mean theater ... and all that." It was odd how many people one met in one's life who at one time or another aspired to the theater. It was like a plague.

"I didn't know you had any connection with the theater," I said sarcastically. "You don't seem to understand the importance of terms like 'integrity of the script.'"

"What the hell does that mumbo jumbo mean?" she asked, her eyes flaring in anger.

"Well, it seems absurd to me that the only reason this case is in Retro is that a toy mouse was found alongside the corpses. Since the toy mouse is still the center of your case, the next steps should concentrate on cats. Right? Mice and cats go together. That's what is meant by 'integrity of the script.'"

"I didn't come here to argue with you," she replied.

"Why did you come here?"

"To ask you if you are losing your mind."

"I think I'm quite sane."

"Sane? Then why are your computer inquiries key-worded with such items as 'leaf bouquets,' 'swamps,' 'crooked pictures,' and a whole lot of other nonsense? You're starting to embarrass a lot of people, Alice. And I thought it was part of our arrangement to keep you on that you maintain a low profile."

"How low?"

"It doesn't matter anymore. I came here now to tell you the arrangement is finished. Just submit your final bill and expenses and we'll pay it."

Her words stunned me. I hadn't expected to be fired. I had thought our differences were all ironed out. Besides, Tony was on his way upstate. Things were beginning to break open.

"Can we postpone this?" I asked gently. "Can you give me another week?"

"Why?"

"Because I have developed something . . . I have found out something."

"That a cat has ten lives?" she asked contemptuously. "Look, Alice . . . Miss Nestleton . . . this has been a big mistake from the beginning. You're lost in some never-never-land and this is basically a police investigation."

"One would never know it," I said gently.

She stared at me angrily. Then she said, "Be out of here in an hour! And remember, the moment you leave these premises today, you no longer have access to Retro data. Don't even try to make inquiries of any kind."

She walked so quickly away that the draft from her departure sent loose papers spinning off my desk. I sat in that cubicle for about an hour without moving. Then the shock wore off and I packed as best I could. When I left the building two hours later I was carrying two stuffed shopping bags. No one said good-bye to me.

The moment I got out onto Centre Street my arms began to tremble. I put the shopping bags down. The weather looked threatening.

I felt little anger. Mostly sadness, a kind of numbing sadness. It wasn't like an acting part I had earned was being denied me. It was more like I had taken an examination and the examiner had failed me because she had misunderstood my answers.

It was the kind of sadness which comes when you realize that the logic of the whole situation was so disjointed that nothing good could come of it.

A familiar figure came in view—threading his way across the street between traffic.

It was Detective Rothwax. I didn't want to see anyone from Retro. I picked up my shopping bags and moved away from the entrance . . . to the uptown side of the building.

But it was too late. He had spotted me. He hesitated as if he couldn't decide to opt for me or the building entrance. Then he chose me.

He walked briskly up to me, stopped about two feet away, and said in an oddly stilted voice, "I'm sorry."

"About what?" I replied.

"We heard that Mizener gave you the boot."

"How could you have heard? It just happened."

He didn't reply to that, but he gave me one of those infuriating cop looks which said he knew things before they happened because he was inside and I was outside and that's the way it always was ... is ... and will be ... that he knew I was going to be fired even before Judy Mizener knew because Judy Mizener wasn't one of them either.

Then he turned away from me so that we were standing next to each other but not looking at each other ... instead, sharing a view of the street.

"You know what I can do?" he asked, making a strange enveloping motion with his hand and then answering his own question. "I can point out the good guys and the bad guys."

He waited for a response from me. There was none.

"I mean, even right now, here, on Centre Street. All these people walking by in front of me. If push comes to shove, I can point out to you the good guys and the bad guys."

"Good for you," I said finally, quietly, a bit sarcastically.

Rothwax pressed on. "That's the difference between you and me. I can read the street and you can't. I know what is going down and you don't. So I get a different perspective ... a different way of looking at things ... and when you start talking—"

"Spare me the tough-cop routine," I said quickly, interrupting. This was getting to be a stupid conversation.

"All I'm saying is that there were bound to be problems."

"Okay."

"It was inevitable that you would irritate a lot of people."

"Oh, come on ... you and your friends got on me the moment I walked into that room. Before anyone had heard anything I had to say."

"Because everyone knew what kind of approach you were going to take."

"You mean they couldn't handle an intelligent approach?"

Rothwax didn't appreciate my quip. I could hear him swear underneath his breath. I realized in some strange sense that he was standing there like that in way of an apology. He was sorry that I had been fired because he didn't like to see anyone fired. It offended his Patrolmen's Benevolent Association's ethic.

"Listen, Detective, there is no doubt that you people are wonderful when it comes to street crimes. You're simply way out of my league. But when it comes to high crimes—"

"When it comes to what?"

"High crimes."

"What the hell is a high crime?"

"Something like the toy-mouse murders. Or ...

let me put it another way—any crime that conceals some kind of grace."

"Now you have lost me completely, lady."

"Well, I lost Judy Mizener. Why shouldn't I lose you?"

He changed the subject. "That detective who recommended you ... what the hell was his name."

"Hanks," I reminded him.

"Right. Hanks. Well, he told me you'd be a problem. He told me straight out."

"Oh, did he? Poor Detective Hanks. Did you know that he also thought I was a fool at the beginning? Did you know that?"

"I don't know nothing about you and Detective Hanks, lady."

"Well, he didn't think I was a fool at the end of the investigation, though. Oh, yes, Detective Hanks was a splendid street cop like yourself. He was really down and dirty. The trouble was that, although he was the first police officer on the scene after a grisly shooting in an East Village bar ... although he had access to all the evidence and all the eyewitness testimony, when push came to shove every bit of his brilliant street cop's report was wrong. He said it was a drug deal gone wrong. There were no drugs involved at all. He said it was A. It turned out to be B. He said C. It turned out to be D. He said apples. It turned out to be oranges. He thought the murder was about money. It turned out to be about a white cat. Do you understand, Detective Roth-wax?"

"A white cat? No, I don't understand."

"How about a whole string of white cats?"

"You've lost me."

"How about a line of white cats that originated in the Moscow Art Theater? How about a line of white cats that people would murder for?"

"Calm down, lady. Calm down," he said, moving away from me a bit.

"I am calm."

"No ... you're spinning your wheels. All I'm saying is that the whole deal went bad the first time you stepped into Retro."

"Was that my fault? Was it my fault a bunch of juveniles started making catcalls?"

"You should have been prepared for it. You shouldn't have let it bother you."

"Well, thank you for your advice, Detective."

We were silent for a while. But Detective Roth-wax didn't leave. And I didn't move. I wondered where Detective Arcenaux was. I wondered if he, too, knew that I had been fired.

"And I'll tell you something else ..." he finally said, then paused, removed a roll of cough drops from his shirt pocket, offered me one, which I refused, and popped one into his mouth with a benevolent sigh, as if the world was now set right. "I think your theories are crazy. But I also think everything in that Retro blue book on the case is Grade A manure."

"You mean the computer is inaccurate?"

"No . . . no . . . forget the computer. I mean I'm beginning to think that the toy-mouse connection is a scam. I don't think there is any connection between the murders at all. Nothing . . . nada."

For some reason, he spat the cough drop out onto the street.

"You know," he said, "when I was a kid, I had a cat."

"That's nice," I said. It came out sarcastic but I hadn't meant it that way. I just didn't know how to respond. So what if he had a cat when he was a child? A lot of people do.

"But my mother made me get rid of him."

"Why?"

"She was allergic to cats."

"And you've been tormented ever since," I teased.

"No. The cat had to go."

"You mean like I had to go?"

"Sort of."

"You mean I gave you people a rash?"

He got huffy. "Okay. All I wanted to say was I was sorry the way the whole stupid thing turned out." And then he walked toward the building entrance and vanished through the swinging doors.

The shopping bags were so heavy that I decided to take a cab back to my apartment, and the moment I got into the cab the heavens opened and torrents of spring rain poured down. The cab crawled uptown through the rain. A block from my apartment the rain suddenly ceased and by the time I left the cab the sun was out again.

I dragged my shopping bags up the stone steps, opened the outer door, and stepped into the vestibule, searching for my keys.

A man's hand reached out and touched my arm! Frightened, I dropped one of the shopping bags and stepped back against the door. The hand dropped away.

I turned and stared. Then I screamed. In front of me was the most horrible face I had ever seen—crisscrossed with white stripes.

"God! Shut up, Alice. It's me. Tony."

I froze halfway toward the second scream. Yes, it was Tony. And those things on his face were bandages.

# 14

It took us hours to get into my apartment. We crawled up the stairs. I kept on dropping the shopping bags because I had to hold on to a wavering Tony.

When we finally got into the apartment I deposited Tony on the sofa and dropped the bags heavily to the floor.

I sat down on the floor, exhausted.

The phone started to ring. It rang and rang. I realized that I hadn't connected the answering device. The phone stopped ringing.

Then Bushy began to act strangely. He walked back and forth with his tail high and started to make very odd sounds.

"I scare him," Tony whispered.

Maybe he did. I didn't know. I stared at Tony. His face was like hamburger with all kinds of absurd white patches over it, as if he had been treated by a madman. His wrists and fingers were also bandaged.

Then I rushed into the kitchen and returned with a glass of apple juice. I fed it to him like he was a baby.

"They fired me, Tony," I said to him, talking

as if he was a sick child who had to be diverted from some horrible truth.

He smiled and almost choked. It was very hard for him to swallow the liquid.

"God, Tony," I finally blurted out, "tell me what happened."

He nodded and pushed the juice away.

The phone started to ring again. I remained where I was. Weakly Tony raised one hand to signify that I should answer it. I let it ring. Bushy leapt up on the dining-room table, his tail still high. I stared at him. Bushy never went onto the dining-room table. Never. That was where Pancho rested from time to time.

The phone stopped again. Tony smiled weakly.

"What happened, Tony?" I persisted. His face was so strange, filled with those small white bandages.

"I rented a car. A Toyota Tercel. I started driving up to the Adirondacks ... to Desolate Swamp." His hand dropped the apple-juice glass and it fell onto the carpet. Bushy leapt down from the table, inspected the mess, then scooted across the room to the window ledge.

"I'm sorry, Swede."

"What happened, Tony?"

"I reached Kingston. That's about two hours north of here, at the turnoff for Route Twenty-eight."

He paused and tried to catch his breath. The phone was still ringing in my ears but it had stopped.

"I remember there was an overpass and traffic suddenly slowed down. I was in the middle lane. And there was a truck tailgating me so I moved to the speed lane. Then suddenly I heard these crazy noises ... like tiny little explosions that rang in my ear ... and then all the glass in my windshield began to shatter and fly around."

He leaned back and closed his eyes. He looked in pain. I moved to the sofa beside him and ran my hand through his hair.

"Someone shot at me from the overpass. With a deer rifle, the cops said. They said I was lucky to be alive. Once the glass started shattering, I turned the wheel and ran up on the center retainer. Luckily, my car stalled there, otherwise it would have gone over to the south lane and I would have been crushed by oncoming traffic. Anyway, they took me to the emergency ward, but all I had was a lot of tiny cuts ... hundreds of them ... on my face and hands ... and I lost a lot of blood."

The phone started to ring again. This time I picked it up. The conversation was very bizarre.

"Is this Alice Nestleton? ... My name is Tricia Lamb. Your agent gave me your name. I'm producing Sophocles' *Philoctetes* in New York this coming winter."

Silence. I stared at Tony.

"Do you hear me?"

"Yes, yes," I replied.

"Well, I'd like to meet with you."

"For what?"

"Concerning your appearing in the production."

The whole conversation was confusing me. I kept staring at Tony. He seemed to be in pain. He kept trying to move on the sofa.

"Can we meet tomorrow? Around one? For lunch? There's a nice Japanese restaurant on Forty-sixth, just west of Fifth. It's called Datsu."

"What did you say your name was?"

"Tricia Lamb. I assure you, this is a production that will interest you."

And then she hung up.

"Who was it?"

"A woman named Tricia Lamb."

I laughed out loud and then tried to explain. "She's a producer. She wants to offer me a role in *Philoctetes.*"

"In what?"

*"Philoctetes.* That play by Sophocles. At least I think that's why she called."

I sat back down beside Tony. I understood that I had made a lunch appointment with the strange caller, but it seemed to be very unreal. The caller, my cats, myself, Tony—all of us seemed to be suspended over a precipice, and beneath us, shrouded in a fog so thick we could not see, was the Desolate Swamp. All kinds of things began to pop into my head—names, places, events.

Then I buried my face in my hands and began to sob. I could not stop crying. It was like someone was inside of me and pushing the tears out.

Tony picked up my hand. "What is the matter

with you? Why are you crying like that? What is wrong with you?" He kept repeating his questions over and over again.

When I had finally stopped, when I finally could keep the sobs down, I became furious at him for some reason. "Don't you understand? I almost got you killed!" I was screaming at him. The noise sent Bushy scurrying away and brought Pancho in from some high crag in the kitchen to confront the enemy.

"Calm down, Swede, you're getting crazy. Yes, I could have been killed. But I wasn't. Calm down."

"Look at your face, Tony!"

"It will heal. Believe me, Swede, it will heal."

"I know who shot you, Tony."

"Who?"

"That madman—Karl Bonaventura."

"You don't have any proof of that, Swede."

"Proof? The man is psychotic. And I'll tell you something else. Remember when we were in his sister's apartment? Remember he told us about the notes? The notes she wrote her cat on the back of the bills. Well, I think he set the whole thing up. I think he wrote the notes. I think he sent us to the Desolate Swamp so he could murder one of us or both of us."

"I don't know what to make out of what you're saying now, Swede. I'm very tired. Really, I'll talk about it with you later."

I helped him lie down on the sofa. I rushed into

the hall closet and brought back pillows and blankets and tried to make him comfortable.

Then I stepped back and stared out the window. It was astonishing. There was still daylight left. I had already lost my job ... been offered a role in a play ... discovered that someone had tried to murder Tony—and there was still daylight left. It was hard to comprehend.

# 15

I spent the next morning taking care of Tony ...
rereading Sophocles' *Philoctetes*, which I had in
a very beat-up old paperback, and in what was
probably a very outdated translation ... and
thinking with great bitterness about Judy Mizener and Retro—about being cut off from an op-
portunity to help seventeen murdered souls rest
in peace. It was odd, I realized, how every bit of
evidence I had brought to Retro's computer for
evaluation had further alienated Retro's staff
from me. It was they who had made the original
connection between all the murders—the toy
mouse. But the more I confirmed their original
insight, the more I showed them that the crime
was indeed in some very profound sense feline,
the more they had backed away.

Tony was still in a kind of shock, lying on the
sofa, then walking about the apartment, then going back to the sofa. He carried on long, rather
obscure conversations with Bushy, who looked
upset that his usual morning siesta was constantly being interrupted by this interloper.

I was fifteen minutes late for my appointment
in the Japanese restaurant with Tricia Lamb. She

was not at all what I had expected. I mean, she had told me she was producing the play, so I anticipated a producer type. But she turned out to be one of those strange fringe people who keep popping up and vanishing in the theater. She wore jeans and a lovely white sweater. No makeup, no ornaments, a face so pale it looked like a piece of papyrus. She spoke in a conspiratorial hush and her accent sounded vaguely Bostonian. It was impossible to tell her age. She could have been twenty-five. She could have been fifty.

I had a bottle of Japanese beer. She ordered and drank three vodka martinis before I ordered broiled eel on a bed of rice. I like eel. She ordered only a cup of clam soup and an endive salad.

We made small talk until the food came. Then she said, "I saw your performance in Montreal— the Portabello production of *Romeo and Juliet.* You were spectacular."

"Thank you."

"I think what we're doing will intrigue you. Do you know the play?"

"I've read it. I never saw a production."

She smiled almost maliciously and leaned forward over the table. Her eyes were glinting amber. "I've been obsessed with this play a long time. A very long time."

It was not the kind of statement one could respond to. I started to pick at the eel and rice.

"Do you have a theater?" I asked.

"No theater ... a loft on Leonard Street ... downtown."

For most actresses, the word "loft" signals death—an amateur production ... not worthy of professionalism. But not for me. I have been alive long enough to know that nothing good happens in New York theater unless it is in a loft ... the grimier the better.

"Who is directing?"

"Me," she said in a violent whisper. "I'm producing and directing and funding, and my translation of the play is the one being used."

That was strange. "Did you study Greek?"

"I studied everything."

She drank her soup fastidiously, down to the last drop. Then she prepared to eat the salad. But she put the fork down.

"The play is not what it seems," she said. "It seems to be about a Greek archer on his way to Troy. He is bitten by a snake and the wound becomes infected and painful. The stench from the wound and the man's cries are too much for his comrades to bear ... so they abandon him on a deserted island. He survives there but his wound will not heal. Meanwhile, his comrades cannot capture Troy. An oracle is given to them. Troy will be conquered only if Philoctetes is rescued from his island and brought to Troy. But Philoctetes refuses to be rescued if it means going to Troy, for his hatred of his comrades is too strong. He wants them to be defeated."

She smiled, picked up one piece of salad, and

let it drop back into the plate. Then she continued.

"Only when the demigod Heracles is sent down to the island does Philoctetes agree to go. Scholars say the play is about the conflict between the individual and the state ... or how one must sacrifice one's own feelings—either likes or dislikes—for the good of the many ... in this case the need for the Greeks to conquer Troy."

"And what do you think?"

"I think that's nonsense. I think the play is about the wound."

"I don't understand."

"It's about a wound that will not heal ... a wound that becomes increasingly loathsome. It's about existence."

I understood vaguely what she was talking about and I sympathized. But while she was speaking, all I could think of was Karl Bonaventura. About his wound. About the festering memory of a dead sister that seemed to have pushed him into attempted murder.

"You see, Alice, in my translation of the play, the wound is in the groin, not in the foot. The wound is castration. The wound is impotence. And all the roles, except for the lead, except for the hero with the wound, are played by women."

That was unexpected. I snapped out of my Bonaventura musing and paid Tricia Lamb more attention. I had thought, when she originally contacted me, that I would be merely passing myself off as a man in a man's role. After all, many actresses have played Hamlet in drag. Just as many men have played women's roles. But Tricia Lamb was literally changing the sex of the protagonists, except for Philoctetes.

"Yes," she affirmed, noticing my surprise, "an all-female cast, playing women, even the chorus—except for Philoctetes."

"Have you altered the script to make that more logical?" I asked.

"I have done a lot of things with the script but I have more or less kept the framework of the play intact—at least in terms of dialogue."

The waiter took away our plates. She had not finished her salad. I had eaten every scrap of the eel and most of the rice. I ordered ice cream for dessert.

"I think the role of Odysseus would be perfect for you. I truly do."

"Odysseus?"

"Yes."

I ate my ice cream slowly. Tricia Lamb was now staring past me . . . as if she was envisioning opening night.

"Don't you want any dessert?" I asked her.

"No," she replied. "Actually, I don't like Japanese food. The only reason I go to Japanese restaurants for lunch is I like the plain wooden tables they always use." She ran her hand over the polished wood grain.

"When do you need an answer?"

"Well, there's plenty of time. I hope we'll start previews sometime next February or March. And rehearsal in early December. Actually, there's going to be a kind of workshop first before we get into the script."

"What kind of workshop?"

"Just a kind of study session so everyone involved knows where I'm coming from . . . so they know what I see is going on . . . so they can deal with their *wound.*" She looked at me slyly and grinned.

"I'll think it over very carefully," I said to her.

"Good! I want you very much in the role. I love your work!"

"Well, thank you."

"I know that I haven't been too precise . . . that I have been talking in vague concepts a lot. But I'll send you my translation in a couple of weeks. Don't make any decision until you read it."

"It's a short play, isn't it?"

"Well, I guess so. It depends to a great extent how we use the chorus."

"And the chorus also will be women?"

"Yes. As I already said, the only male part played by a male will be Philoctetes."

"What about dress? Contemporary?"

"I haven't decided."

"But not Greek?"

"No, no togas."

"Well, as long as we're not nude," I said. And Tricia Lamb threw back her head and laughed. At that moment, staring at this woman, I thought of the cat Abelard. I don't know why. It was just the way Tricia Lamb moved. I had the weird feeling that if I ever got to see Abelard during my cat-sitting visits, he would look like her—that is, Abelard the cat would look like Tricia Lamb the producer. Maybe I wasn't used to the Kirin beer. Or maybe I was having a blood-sugar explosion from the pistachio ice cream.

The waiter brought the check. Tricia Lamb studied it for a while, took out a credit card, put it back, took out cash, then put the bills back, produced the credit card again, and paid with that.

She smiled at me. It made me uncomfortable. It was the kind of smile that said I was wise and wonderful and much older than she. She didn't know I had forgotten all my lines when it came to seventeen murders and seventeen toy mice and clues that were laughed at and interpretations that were considered bizarre and a dear, dear friend whom I almost sent to his death.

"I'm going downtown. Can I drop you off in a cab?" she asked.

"No, thanks. I think I'll walk."

We had finished our business and finished our food and the bill was paid but neither of us made a move to leave. It was probably loneliness. Theater people on the fringe are very lonely. We have lost our theater friends.

"Did you know a New York actor named Bill Lukens?" she asked.

"I don't think so."

"He was in New York about ten years ago. He used to do one-man shows downtown."

"No, I didn't know him. Why do you ask?"

"No reason. I knew him. We lost contact." Her brief explanation hid about every bad love story one would ever read about.

"What kind of stuff did he do?"

"It was pretty way-out. A combination of mime and song. He had a beautiful voice."

"Where downtown?"

"I don't remember."

It was so odd sitting there making that kind of delicious small talk when I knew that poor Tony was recovering on my sofa under the baleful eyes of Bushy.

"He studied at the Yale Drama School," she said.

"A nice place," I noted, with a little twist of sarcasm.

"A nice guy for a nice place."

"Was he wounded?"

She laughed out loud. "Yes. He was Philoctetes."

"But who isn't? Right?"

She nodded and her face grew grim and for a moment I thought she was going to cry. But she didn't.

"Let's go," she said. We got up and walked out of the restaurant.

"Here's my phone and my address. But I'll send you the translation first. Read it. Think about it. Then give me a decision." We shook hands like businessmen. How odd.

\* \* \*

It was eight o'clock that evening. Tony lay on my sofa; he seemed to be much better, though it was now obvious he wouldn't win any facial beauty contests for a long time to come. I was sitting at the long wood table across the room. Bushy was out of sight, probably in my bedroom, on the pillow, protecting his space because he was nervous that Tony would requisition it.

On the floor beside the sofa lay a half-eaten chicken-salad sandwich and an empty wineglass that had been one-third filled with Martell's.

"Tony, I want to read you something. A passage from *Philoctetes.*"

"Sure, Swede, read away."

"The chorus is speaking about our hero. 'I marvel how he kept his hold upon a life so full of woe . . . with no living soul in the land to be near him while he suffered . . . no compassionate ear into which he could pour forth the lament, awakening response, for the plague that gnawed the flesh and drained his blood . . . no one to soothe, with healing herbs, the burning pus oozing from his ulcerated foot. All he can do is creep with painful steps—"

"Enough, Swede, enough!" Tony interrupted. "The man has a problem. I agree."

I closed the book. "Who does it remind you of, Tony?"

"Quasimodo."

I ignored that comment. "Karl Bonaventura."

"His feet seemed perfectly healthy to me."

"The wound is in his heart. The death of his

sister. Or maybe the death of the sister was an attempt to heal his wound. Maybe an incestuous wound."

"What the hell are you saying, Swede? First of all, I don't even believe that it was Karl who shot at me from that overpass. And you seem to be taking it a bit further."

"Yes. I am."

"Look, Swede. I think you're starting to lose control here. Because you can't accept one fact."

"Which is?"

"That you're not one step closer to solving those murders than you were at the beginning. All you came up with was a lot of funny little facts. Like some of the pictures on the walls of the victims were crooked; like a Mother Goose nursery rhyme; like most of the cats seem to have vanished at the time of the murders ..." He stopped speaking for a moment, reached down for the glass, saw that it was empty, made a face, and continued: "Like a swamp somewhere in the Adirondacks. Look, Swede, the fact is that you haven't done any better than those computer whizzes at Retro."

I was angry. But I kept my voice down. "You forget the space between the crimes ... and the seasons. They have to be cat-related."

"Well, it wasn't you, Swede, who came up with those figures. You told me it was the FBI agent from Baltimore. But look, nothing you came up with is any more substantial than what Retro came up with ... toy mice in dead people's apartments. God, Swede, this is all crazy."

"You sound just like Judy Mizener."

"I sound like a man with a battered face who needs another brandy."

I went to the kitchen, brought back the bottle, and gave him a little more brandy. I also took some for myself in a coffee cup, the way my grandmother used to drink it on cold evenings when she was bedding down her dairy cows for the night.

"Tony," I said gently after I took the first sip, "I think we went to the wrong apartment."

"What are you talking about?"

"We shouldn't have gone to Jill Bonaventura's apartment ... that's just a shrine. We should have gone to Karl's apartment."

"Why?"

"That's where we would have found something important."

"But you thought that slip of paper was important at the time. Or you wouldn't have sent me on that crazy trip to the Desolate Swamp."

"I told you before. Karl probably forged that. To kill you ... or both of us. He knew we would follow it up. He wants us out of the way."

"Why? Do you think he killed his sister? Man, the guy is psychotic from grief." He sat up and looked at me wide-eyed. "Or do you think he killed the others?"

I took another sip of the brandy. It was spring

in New York. I usually drank brandy only in the winter. How old-fashioned I am.

"A lot of things were going through my mind during lunch with that producer, Tony. A lot of things."

"You mean you discovered that Karl Bonaventura is a reincarnated Philoctetes. What would Sophocles think about that? He wrote the goddamn play."

"Be serious, Tony. We have a lot of dead people to care for." My comment bit into him. He cursed under his breath and lay back down on the sofa.

"Just relax and listen, Tony. Okay? Just hear me out. First of all, there are really only two pieces of information that seemingly have nothing to do with the murders. The first is those damn leaf bouquets that I found in Jack Tyre's apartment."

"You mean the valentines from that lady?"

"Right. And the second is what Karl Bonaventura told us about his sister. The money."

"What money?"

"The twenty-five hundred dollars he said she asked for the year of her death and the two years previously."

"I remember."

"Two pieces of information. Two things. And both of them are decidedly unfeline. They seem to be outside of the case. Like burrs on a tail."

"I think, Swede, you're around the bend. Who ever heard of assigning importance to evidence because it *doesn't* fit in with any other evidence? It's sort of a bizarre criterion."

"Well, I'm doing it anyway. And I'm taking it one step further. I have this strange feeling that Karl Bonaventura and Georgina Kulaks know each other."

"But they don't."

"How do we know?"

"What you are really telling me, Swede, is that you have this crazy intuition that they have become, in your mind, prime suspects."

"If the shoes fits, Tony, wear it."

"There is no shoe. There is no fit."

"Let's go to Bonaventura's apartment."

"It's not an apartment. It's a small house in Sheepshead Bay, Brooklyn."

"Well, let's pay him a visit. Let's look the place over. Let's see what we can find."

He swung his legs over and sat up again, throwing up his hands in despair. "Don't you see how crazy you're talking, Swede? You're telling me that Karl and that woman Kulaks are in cahoots because each of them is connected to a piece of irrelevant evidence. Your logic is crazy."

"We have nothing to lose, Tony."

"Why don't you just accept the fact that Retro fired you and this case is beyond you and me and the whole goddamn police department?"

"Let me be the judge of that," I replied.

"I'm talking too much, Swede. My face is starting to hurt."

"Call Karl Bonaventura, Tony."

He stared at me angrily for what seemed the longest time. Then he sighed wearily, took out his wallet, extracted a card, and walked to the phone. He dialed. He listened for a while. Then he hung up the receiver.

"There was a message on his answering service. He'll be away for a few days. Just leave your name and phone number and he'll return the call as soon as he gets back."

He walked back to the sofa and sat. I smiled broadly.

"What are you grinning at?" he asked. "I did what you told me."

"Tell me, Tony. What is the iron law of life in New York in regard to the telephone?"

"You tell me."

"Thou shalt not leave a message on your answering machine that you will be away for a few days. It is an open invitation to thieves."

"Well, Bonaventura is not an intelligent psychotic," Tony replied.

"Or maybe he went up to that overpass in Kingston to blow you away. And he had to give himself a couple of days' leeway to stand on the overpass to make sure he got you."

"Assuming that he followed me to the car-rental place and knew what kind of car I rented," Tony replied skeptically.

"Yes, assuming that. And then he decided to break the iron law because he knew his compatriot would call and he wanted her to rest easy, knowing that he was taking care of business."

"His compatriot being Georgina Kulaks, I imagine. Oh, hell, Swede, this is really stretching it. Why would these two people murder seventeen innocent men and women? Including their loved ones."

"Humor me, Tony. Let's go to Sheepshead Bay."

"But he's not back yet from wherever he went."

"I know that. So what?"

Tony took another sip of brandy. He looked at me suspiciously.

"Are you saying what I think you're saying?"

"What am I saying?"

"That we should break in."

"Yes."

"I'm a law-abiding citizen, Swede. I may have left my wife and children. I may have delusions of theatrical grandeur at an advanced age. I may be throwing my copying business down the drain. But I'm not a thief."

"Neither am I," I responded.

"Then what do you call it?"

"I call it a necessity."

Bushy had ambled back into the living room, tail up. He walked to the half-eaten chicken sandwich on the carpet, sniffed it, and turned away. Then he sniffed the brandy. He didn't like that either. He stretched, sat down, turned his large lovely head in my direction, and gave me one of his unfathomable stares.

"Even your cat thinks you're crazy," Tony said.

"My cat, Tony," I corrected him, "thinks I am a good woman with very loyal friends."

"You see, this is what happens when you confide in people. If I hadn't bared my soul to you, Swede, and told you that at a certain point in my disheveled childhood I was rather expert at breaking into cars, you never would have brought this damn thing up."

"Do you have any cash on you, Tony?"

"Some," he said warily.

"It's about ten dollars to Brooklyn, isn't it?"

"More like twenty-five, Swede. That's the tip of Brooklyn." He paused. "When do you want to go?"

"Now, Tony, now!"

He looked very sad.

"What's the matter, Tony?" I asked, suddenly concerned about his sadness.

I sat down beside him on the sofa and my right hand touched his bruised cheekbone for just a moment. Then I pulled my hand away but stayed close—our legs touching.

"Swede, if you want me to take you to Bonaventura's house in Brooklyn, I'll do it. If you want me to break in, I'll do it. If you want me to go upstate again, I'll do it. Whatever you want me to do, I'll do. But you're going to have to start being honest with me."

"About what, Tony? How have I been dishonest?"

"About what you feel for me."

"It's hard to talk about," I replied.

"Since when are you shy, Swede?"

"Maybe you don't know me as well as you think."

"Obviously."

"Why are you getting mad, Tony?"

He pushed me away from him suddenly, stood up, and walked across the room to the window that fronted the street.

He turned. "I want to know what's going on. We make wild passionate love in a hotel room and it's just like it never happened. You start treating me like I'm your brother or your secretary—not your lover."

"You are my brother, Tony ... and my friend and my helper and my lover—you're all those things to me, I think, Tony. Why do you need definition now? Why do you need confirmation?"

"Why? Because nothing is happening."

"What should be happening?"

"I don't know. But something more. Look, Swede, remember when you came to my hotel room and we made love? Remember how bad I looked, how confused I was, how distraught because I had left my wife and kids to go back to a life that had crushed me once before? Well, after we made love that time, I was no longer frightened. Everything was going to be okay."

He laughed one of his silly laughs, a self-mocking laugh that made me very uncomfortable.

"And then," he charged dramatically, "you withdrew."

"I didn't withdraw, Tony. You're forgetting about Jill Bonaventura's apartment, aren't you? We made love there."

"Anecdotal evidence," he replied wickedly. "And that kind of evidence doesn't change the fact that you've withdrawn."

"I hate that word, Tony. It sounds like I'm some sort of official injection. Like insulin. Like I'm either injected or withdrawn."

"Well, what would you call it?"

"Other things are happening."

"People get murdered every day, Swede."

"Don't pressure me, Tony."

"I'm not pressuring you. I'm just trying to get a rational explanation."

I walked to the window and stood beside him. We were both on edge, upset. I didn't want to talk any more about him and me. I didn't want to make love with him. But I also didn't want him angry. Not now. I needed him for a lot of reasons.

"Tony, did it ever occur to you that we're both middle-aged people who keep trying to recreate a postadolescent romantic fantasy. But no matter where or how we look, it simply isn't there."

"I'm not interested in theory, Swede. Why aren't we sleeping together now? Right now. Get it? Okay. I'll take you to Brooklyn later on . . . to that lunatic's house. Okay? But let's go to bed now."

I shook my head.

"Yes," he said bitterly, "that's precisely what

I'm talking about. Why has this almighty NO surfaced? When there had been that wonderful YES. Can't you just tell me the truth? Or maybe you've been hanging out with cops too much and everything comes out in the form of a report—like Retro."

"It is very hard to describe, Tony."

"Well ... do you desire me when I'm gone?"

"Sometimes."

"What determines 'sometimes'?"

"I don't know, Tony."

"I desire you all the time, Swede."

"Maybe it's these awful murders."

"And maybe it's the weather," he retorted bitterly.

"What do you want me to do, Tony? Fake it? Lie about it? I'm trying to tell you the truth. The whole thing is as confusing to me as it is to you. Sometimes I want you. Sometimes I don't."

"Sex as strawberries—in season, out of season."

I was starting to get angry at him. "If it's too much to bear, just leave," I said.

"That's fine with me," he shouted. "I'm sick of playing these goddamn detective games."

He took three ferocious steps toward the door. Then he stopped suddenly in his tracks.

"I'm going to calm down," he said ruefully, "my face is beginning to hurt." He laughed at himself and ran his fingers softly over the bruises.

"Let's both calm down."

"We need a script," he said, chuckling.

"Right. We could never improvise."

"We need a script by a one-legged forty-two-year-old playwright who supports himself by selling T-shirts in front of Carnegie Hall and is desperately in love with a ballet dancer who supports herself by riding an elephant in the circus. The elephant's name is ..." He paused and cocked his head.

"Alice," I offered.

"No, too American."

"Greta."

"Too European."

"Honey."

"Too hard to remember."

"Lutzi."

"Now, that's a beautiful name. How the hell did you think of that, Swede?"

"I don't know. I think there was a friend of my grandmother's named Lutzi, but I don't know how to spell it."

"What does it matter. It's an elephant's name."

"I like the plot, Tony."

"What plot?"

"The one your one-legged playwright is going to come up with."

"So do I."

"It'll be sort of working-class romantic."

"Exactly."

"Like you."

"Exactly. Being torn to pieces by unrequited love and a copying business I can't seem to get rid of."

I walked up to him. We locked hands and went back to the sofa, sitting down in unison like an old farm couple.

Bushy picked up his tail in a huff and moved to the geographic center of the carpet.

Tony grasped my hand tightly. "Swede, do you remember that first term we knew each other in the Dramatic Workshop?"

"Tony . . . that must have been around 1971."

"Probably . . . twenty years at least. But do you remember that workshop performance we did? A sort of abbreviated script based on Arthur Koestler's *Darkness at Noon.*"

"No. I don't."

"It's about a devoted Communist arrested during the Soviet purges. He's brainwashed into confessing he was a traitor."

"I know the story, Tony, it's just that I don't remember the production."

"Sure . . . you must remember. It was during the summer term and the air conditioning broke down."

The bell rang in my head. I did remember. Of course I remembered it. "And they brought in that huge prehistoric fan which was like a plane propeller and the minute it was turned on it blew all kinds of paper out the window," I recalled, and we both laughed at the memory of absurd notes flying down onto Broadway.

"Do you remember the set I designed for that performance?"

"Vaguely. It was like a blanket. Right?"

"An enormous horse blanket. I stretched it across the stage. It was very beat-up. And then I stenciled an enormous hammer and sickle on the blanket in brilliant red ... but I obscured half of the design. And that was the entire set."

"Now I remember."

"It was obvious even then that I was a genius."

"Of course."

"I mean, the set overwhelmed the stage ... the actors ... the whole damn building."

"It was cosmic, Tony."

"Sure," he continued, his eyes glinting with playfulness, pride, self-mockery, "thirty-two people were overcome the moment the curtain went up."

"There was no curtain," I reminded him, "and the entire audience was less than nine."

"Well ... the whole point being that I have always been addicted to the Obscure. And, as we both know, Swede, the obscure, done well, can overwhelm all common sense."

"Are you making a point about me, Tony?" I asked, laughing.

He leaned forward and pressed his lips against my neck. The touch of his mouth was warm. But it wasn't eros. It was need. It suddenly dawned on me that he, Tony, needed me as much as I needed him. I needed his help. He needed my obscurity. I needed his body sometimes. He needed my love sometimes. I was his mother. He was my father. We were both our own children. It was all so confused that none of it meant a damn thing. Then his mouth moved between my breasts. I opened my blouse. My fingers went through his hair, pulling him closer. Brooklyn could wait a bit.

# 16

It was a long bumpy ride into and through Brooklyn to Sheepshead Bay. The cab dropped us off on a deserted street with no streetlights visible. The street was lined on both sides with small one-family houses set very close to each other. The houses seemed to squat onto the ground. They had once been just wooden frame dwellings but at some point in time most of them had been given shingles or stone fronts.

I followed Tony, who was moving slowly up one side of the street, peering at the houses to find the numbers. Finally he pointed. "Twenty-three-oh-five. That's the number. That's it." Bonaventura's house had bluish shingles; at least they seemed that color in the night.

"Now what do we do?" Tony asked.

"We walk up to the front door and ring the bell," I said.

So we did that. There was no answer. I rang again and then kept my hand on the buzzer for a long time.

"Now what do we do?" Tony asked.

"You take out your Swiss Army knife. You pull out that funny little pick from the side. You put

it in the keyhole and try to get the door open," I
replied, turning the doorknob to emphasize my
instructions for an increasingly reluctant Tony.

The door popped open! We both stared at it.
"Maybe," Tony said, "other thieves beat us to it."

We walked inside, closed the door behind us,
and switched the hall light on. It was nothing
like his sister's apartment shrine. It was a series
of dingy little rooms which led into a back
kitchen. Karl Bonaventura had obviously spent a
lot of time turning his dead sister's apartment
into a shrine while ignoring his own place or sac-
rificing it.

"What happens if he just shows up?" Tony
asked.

"Well, we came to see him. We rang the bell.
There was no one home but the door was open
so we were afraid he had been burglarized . . . so
we came in."

I started in the living room and proceeded to
search the entire room carefully. I looked in and
under every object. I checked all the framed pictures on the walls—none of them were crooked
and none of them had anything taped to them.
Tony watched me from an easy chair, clearly be-
lieving that he had fulfilled his entire responsibility just by getting me there and into the house.

There was nothing of interest in the living
room. I moved into the long hallway. More pictures on the wall. I longed for a crooked one but
they were straight and true. I went through the
small dingy cabinets that lined the hall. There

were tools and tablecloths and old newspapers, but no leaf bouquets. Nothing.

There were two bedrooms, one on each side of the hall—small, cramped bedrooms, each of which contained a single narrow bed, a single chest, and no pictures at all.

I walked into the west bedroom and sat down for a moment on the narrow bed. The mattress was tight and springy, as if it had rarely been slept on.

"Do you smell anything?" Tony asked. He was standing in the hallway.

I sniffed the air. There was a faint odor in the house.

"It's stronger in the kitchen," he said.

"Maybe he left a gas jet on when he left," I said.

"No, it's not gas," Tony replied.

We both walked into the kitchen, which was the last room in the small house, with a door opening onto the backyard. The kitchen was in disarray—pots and pans and cartons on the tables and chairs. There was a badly dripping sink faucet.

"For a guy who fixes cars for a living, you'd think he'd be able to fix his faucet," Tony noted.

"Our psychotic friend has other things on his mind."

"Maybe that's why he became psychotic . . . the Chinese water torture—drip, drip, drip."

I opened the refrigerator. Maybe it was spoiled

food. The refrigerator was empty except for two macaroni-and-cheese dinners in the freezer.

"Damn! This place has a basement," Tony exclaimed. He walked to the tall narrow door that I had thought was a closet when I first saw it. There was a light just inside the door. Tony flicked it on.

We started gingerly down the unsteady staircase. The smell was heavier now.

We never got to the bottom of the stairs. Our vision was suddenly blotted out.

Hanging from a twisted rope at the bottom of the stairs was the decomposing body of Karl Bonaventura.

The rope had been attached to a fixture in the ceiling. Then he must have climbed to the top of the stairs and jumped forward. The body was turning slowly.

I ran back up the stairs and into the kitchen. Clenching my fists, I leaned against the wall. Tony came up after me. We looked at each other and said nothing for a long while.

Finally Tony asked: "Should we call 911?"

"Why call anyone? What does it matter?" Then I dimly reconsidered. "We'll call before we leave."

Tony sat down wearily on one of the kitchen chairs. "Swede," he said softly, "I'm afraid this knocks all your theories to hell. He's been dead awhile. That's why the body smells. He must have killed himself right after he left us in his sister's apartment. He must have come home and

135

hanged himself. And that means it wasn't Karl who shot at me."

"Let's get out of here, Tony," I said. He nodded his head in agreement. But neither of us moved. My legs were still rubbery. I closed my eyes. Philoctetes was dead. He could no longer stand the pain of his wound.

Two hours later Tony and I were sitting dumbly in my apartment. It was between two and three in the morning. All the lights were out. Some light did filter in through the windows from the street.

Bushy was in my arms. He wasn't too happy there but he understood that I needed to be comforted. Pancho knew it too—he had stopped his constant flight and was now sitting on the dining table cleaning his right paw. Tony was next to me on the sofa, his eyes closed, his arms behind his neck, and his long legs stretched out.

"Tony," I said, "I'm not going to take the part."

"Why not?"

"Because I have other things on my mind."

"You're deluding yourself. You have nothing else on your mind except getting yourself deeper and deeper into an NYPD case where you're not wanted. And that's unhealthy. Take the part, Swede."

"It would be unseemly," I replied, using a very old-fashioned word.

"What is unseemly?"

"Doing a theater piece in a landscape littered with the murdered."

"You have to start getting hold of yourself, Swede, you're starting to sound like some kind of avenging angel ... like you have a personal responsibility for seventeen corpses. And you're also going to have to accept the fact, Swede, that sooner or later you were going to come face-to-face with a problem you couldn't solve. And it may very well be these murders."

I buried my face in Bushy's extravagant ruff. Then I dropped him back onto the carpet where he wanted to be and walked quickly to the phone and dialed Tricia Lamb's number.

"Swede, it's three o'clock in the morning. Who the hell are you waking?"

But I didn't wake anyone. Her machine was on. I left a simple message. No *Philoctetes* for me at this time. Then I hung up.

As I turned to go back toward the sofa I was suddenly struck by the loveliness of my apartment in the gentle darkness and the creatures in it—Bushy and Pancho and Tony. I stood still. Tony was right. My imagination had gone out of control with poor Karl Bonaventura. I had been acting like an ingenue—all filled with my own glory. As if I believed that the first wild things that rushed into my head were eternally valid. As if my interpretation of the play was so acute, so intuitive, that I could not err.

"Swede, why are you standing there?" I heard Tony ask.

"Just thinking, Tony."

Had I become obsessed with this case to the point of irrationality? Had I slipped into a delusion that I was the Captain Avenger for all those poor people ... for all the sadness of their deaths? Or was it just hurt pride? I mean, in a few short days I had uncovered more hard evidence than all the people and machines in Retro. They had discovered only one thing: that a toy mouse was left at each murder scene. I had found out a lot more. That all of the victims' cats had vanished ... that at least one of the cats had been sent on an incomprehensible journey to Desolate Swamp ... that at least one of the victims had been involved in a love affair characterized by a bizarre valentine of leaves ... that the murderer had left a trail of crooked pictures in the apartments of the victims ... that the time sequence of the murders was related to the mating, gestation, and birth cycle of cats ... that one of the relatives of the victims gave the victim twenty-five-hundred-dollar payments for nothing. And after all these revelations, I knew nothing. Retro knew nothing. Tony knew nothing. The world knew nothing. Yes, my pride was hurt.

I turned and looked at the long table. Pancho was still on it. That was strange. He had never stopped for so long. "Pancho," I whispered to him, "are you ill?" He studied me. How his eyes always glinted! "Do you need help, Pancho?" He went back to his paw. I went back to the sofa.

The night slipped away as we sat on the sofa.

Tony was alternately silent and talkative. When he spoke, it was about a growing guilt he felt at leaving his wife and children and about how he was afraid to go back to them and afraid not to go back to them. All I could say in response was that it was inevitable he would.

I fell asleep, fully clothed, with my head draped over the side of the sofa, like a kitten on a tree limb.

When I awoke, my whole side was cramped. The morning light had flooded the room. Where were Tony and Bushy?

"Just stay there, Swede, and be served," I heard Tony call out from the kitchen. And then he came into the living room with coffee for me. I sipped it.

"You forgot the sugar, Tony."

He went back into the kitchen. I stood up and stretched, walking slowly to the window while rotating my neck.

"Here's the sugar," Tony called out, returning with two packets. He placed them on the dining-room table.

I turned toward him, away from the street scene, and then burst into laughter.

He had brought the sugar packets from the kitchen to the living room with Bushy draped around his neck like a fur stole. Both seemed quite happy with the arrangement.

"I see you two are becoming intimate," I said.

Tony laughed. He pulled gently at Bushy's back feet, which were hanging over his right shoulder.

"I have been asking his advice on various matters."

"Be careful, Tony. Bushy has a very strange sense of humor."

Tony walked back into the kitchen with Bushy. I opened the sugar packets and dumped them into the black coffee. I sat back down on the sofa and sipped the coffee. It was a strange morning. Tony walked back into the living room, Bushy still wrapped around his neck. He held a small bag of garbage in his hand.

"A bouquet for me, Tony?"

"Where do I dump it?"

I stood up, walked to the door, opened it, and pointed into the hallway toward the compactor chute. He carried the bag out and was back in seconds. I closed the door behind him.

"Are you okay, Swede? You look suddenly pale."

I did feel weak.

"Sit down, Swede," Tony said with urgency. I sat back down on the sofa. Tony handed me the cup of coffee. I sipped it.

"Can I get you something?" he asked, letting Bushy climb off his shoulders.

"No, I'll be all right. I was just kind of overwhelmed with a memory."

"What kind of memory?"

"That you and I were lovers."

"Well, we are."

"No, Tony, I meant that we had somehow become another pair of lovers."

"Who?"

"Jack Tyre and Georgina Kulaks."

"You're sounding a bit nutty again, Swede."

I didn't respond. It would be best to say nothing else, I realized. Tony wouldn't understand the connection. He had offered me a bouquet of garbage. Georgina had offered her lover a bouquet of leaves. Tony had walked toward me with a cat draped around his neck. Jack Tyre had walked into the Ramble each weekend with his cat wrapped around his neck.

What had made me weak was the realization that there was such obvious parallels between us and them. It was one of those odd things which are very unnerving for no good reason at all.

"I wonder what the cops are going to do with Karl Bonaventura's body," Tony said.

"Cut him down."

"I mean where he'll be buried?"

I didn't feel like talking about Karl Bonaventura. The horror of seeing his body swinging on those basement stairs was fresh in my memory. And besides, I was still smarting internally from having gotten it all wrong. I mean, it was obvious that Karl Bonaventura could not have attempted to kill Tony at the bypass on the New York Thruway. It was either someone else with a purpose or it was a random shooting. And if it was not Karl, then the slips we found in his sister's apartment were authentic and there was a Desolate Swamp somewhere ... maybe in the woman's mind ... maybe in the Adirondacks ... maybe in Central Park, for all I knew.

"Tell me the truth, Swede, do you want me to go upstate again?"

"Would you, Tony? I thought you were very down on my crime-solving abilities lately."

"Watch what I do, not what I say. Sure, I'll try going up again. But why don't you find a closer Desolate Swamp? Like around the corner." He laughed at his own retort.

"What about Central Park?"

There was something nonjoking in my voice. "Are you serious, Swede?"

Was I serious? Was it worthwhile to follow Jack Tyre into the park ... his beautiful Siamese cat draped over his shoulders? Was there a Desolate Swamp in Central Park? And if so, why would he bring his cat there? For the same reason that Jill Bonaventura sent her cat there?

"I remember you telling me, Swede, about one of the brothers—one of the last victims—who used to take his cat into the park."

"To the Ramble, to be specific," I replied.

"I thought only drug dealers and cruising gays hung out there."

Tony was showing his age. Years ago, the Ramble had had a terrible reputation. It was a dangerous place to walk around in—isolated, heavily wooded, and filled with all kinds of desperate characters. But it had been cleaned up for the bird-watchers, although once in a while one read about the body of a French tourist being found there.

"The Ramble is a big place, Swede, and I never heard of a place called Desolate Swamp there."

"His girlfriend told me Jack Tyre went to a cave."

Tony whooped with sarcasm. "Right, Swede, and it was there that he turned into Batman ... no, Mouseman."

"You don't have to go if you don't want to."

His face turned grim. "Listen, Swede. I will go where you want me to go. That's what I signed on for. All I want you to know and admit is that you're putting more and more hope on facts that are becoming more and more obscure and unimportant. That's all I've been trying to tell you the last few days. That's all I meant when I said you were going around the bend."

"All we're going to do is take a walk in the park, Tony, and trace the route Jack Tyre used to take on those bucolic weekends his ex-lover told me about. That's all, Tony."

Then I dug out of the closet a packet of maps and came up with one I had bought many years ago. It was titled: "The Ramble: A Central Park Walk." And it had a great deal of historical and natural lore as well. I read to Tony the section on the cave.

" 'Under the bridge is a manmade cave, which has been closed for safety reasons since the 1930's. For many years you could row right up to the cave and enter by boat or descend steps cut into the slope beside the cave to get inside. Today the inlet leading to the cave is no longer navigable, it has been silted in with soil washed down the slopes.' "

I handed Tony the map. He looked at it for a few minutes, turning it over in his hands as if it was some complex oceanographic chart.

"Why would Jack Tyre take his cat to play in front of or on top of a sealed cave?"

"I don't know, Tony, that's what we'll find out."

"How desperate you are becoming, Swede."

"I thought you liked desperation, Tony," I chided him.

"Only in bed," he replied.

"Go home now ... I mean go to your hotel. Meet me tomorrow morning in front of the statue at Fifty-eighth and Fifth."

"Which statue? What time?"

"I think it's William Tecumseh Sherman. Make it ten o'clock."

"You're mad at me, Swede."

"Well, you know how it is with us desperate people," I replied sardonically. He kissed me once gently on my neck and left. I was so weary I didn't know what to do next, so I just sat and stared at the map of the Ramble.

# 17

On the one hand it was absurd and on the other hand it was profound. I mean, only an out-of-work actress with a very strong background in fantasy could have gotten upset at noticing a relationship between Tony Basillio and Alice Nestleton on one hand, and Jack Tyre and Georgina Kulaks, on the other hand. Only an out-of-work actress could have discerned the powerful (chuckle) connection between a bouquet of garbage and a bouquet of leaves.

As I was dressing that morning to meet Tony, I knew quite well that I was grasping at straws. So what? Keep grasping!

My head was in a strange place. I was alternately bitter and hopeful . . . nasty and gentle . . . constricted and loose. One moment I prayed that Tony would go back to his family and the next moment I desired him. One moment I was absolutely gleeful that Judy Mizener had fired me from Retro and the next moment it was the biggest failure and disappointment in my life. One moment I knew that I held the secret of the Toy Mouse Murders in my head and heart and the next moment I was a billion miles from even the slightest comprehension of the case.

I stared at myself in the mirror.

I looked strange. Not poorly. Just strange. Or maybe a tiny bit crooked. I laughed. My head was being consumed by the murders. By crooked pictures on walls. By desolate swamps real and imagined.

> He bought a crooked cat,
>   Which caught a crooked mouse,
> And they all lived together
>   In a little crooked house.

My God! What did it all mean? What was nonsense and what was not? I suddenly and savagely began to brush my long hair.

Tony was already there when I arrived. He was not in good humor, obviously angry at himself that he had allowed me to rope him into yet another wild-goose chase. We entered the park at Fifth Avenue and then headed toward the West Drive.

It was a glorious spring morning. Very quickly, all our bad feelings dissipated and we joined arms and walked like we were sashaying lovers. It was so nice, in fact, that I asked Tony if he would mind taking the walking tour of the Ramble with me as outlined in the map I had.

He smiled at me slyly. "I agree with you, Swede. I think we should prolong this cave nonsense as long as possible. Can you imagine what will happen if one of those park cops asks us what we're doing?"

"Just tell the truth, Tony," I replied, "just tell him we're looking for an abandoned cave in which a dead man took his abandoned cat to play in some desolate swamp." It was one of the most absurd things I have ever heard, even if I said it. We both started laughing. It was a fine lark now. I opened the map.

"We have to go back east for a while. The walking tour starts at the Loeb Boathouse."

"Lead on," Tony cried out extravagantly.

Like retarded tourists, we joyously followed the walking tour. First there was the large hemlock, the gateway to the Ramble; then the heavily wooded rock ledge called the Point; then the enormous sink of willows called the Oven. On and on we went, consulting the map every ten feet so we didn't stray from the tour.

The deeper we went into the Ramble, the more isolated we became except for the occasional bird-watcher or homeless person, who passed us without comment.

"How are we doing?" Tony asked, stopping dead in his tracks and signaling that he truly needed a rest.

"Our next stop," I said pedagogically, "is number six—the Rustic Shelter. Then the Gill or Spring."

"And then?"

"And then the Lost Waterfall and then the Lookout."

"Lord . . . when will it all end?"

"Number nine—the cave. Right after the Lookout. Hold on, Tony, we're almost there."

We started walking again and passed a whole colony of homeless who seemed to have established themselves on a wooded slope.

I stopped suddenly.

"What's the matter?" Tony asked.

"It seems that we walked over this stone bridge twice," I replied, confused.

"You can't walk over the same bridge twice," he retorted.

"No, Tony, you have it wrong—the saying is, 'You can't step in the same stream twice.' "

He laughed and kissed me. Then he turned around and leaned against the iron railing, staring out over the Central Park Lake, the shores of which were very close below us.

"Wait a minute," he yelled out. "How about: 'You can't star in the same play twice'? Or: 'You can't climb on the same stage twice'? Or: 'You can't apply the same greasepaint twice'?"

"Calm down, Tony, you're getting out of control," I cautioned him, studying the map carefully. Suddenly I laughed out loud.

"What's the matter with you, Swede?"

"Tony, according to this map, we aren't lost. In fact, this iron railing, the one you're leaning on, is right over the top of the cave."

We both leaned over the iron railing. We were perched over a very large rock structure.

"The opening must be lower," Tony said. We climbed down the side carefully. It was steep but accessible. When we reached the bottom we could see that one of the sides consisted of poured concrete.

"That must have been the opening at one time," I said, kicking the concrete closure gently.

"Let's just walk around it," Tony said. We started to circumnavigate the rock cave. The underbrush became thicker.

"The damn thing is enormous," Tony muttered, kicking at the twisted shrubs. The face of the rock was sheer. There didn't seem to be any other opening at all.

"Maybe crazy Jack used to come here just to sit on it or climb it. Maybe his cat was a rock climber." I ignored Tony's comment and kept moving. We were halfway around it when we saw a pile of beer cans and garbage near the base. We stopped and looked up.

"Swede! Look there!" I stared up at the rock. About twenty feet from the ground was a large dark gash. "It could be a shadow or it could be an opening," I said.

Carefully, slowly, the twigs cutting into our hands and faces, we climbed the steep rock. It was an opening ... but one so narrow that we had to squeeze in with great effort. Tony lit a match. Directly inside were more beer cans and crushed fast-food containers. The homeless had flung their garbage through the opening.

"It looks like it goes deeper," Tony said. He lit another match and we followed the wall.

About twenty yards from that narrow entrance the cave opened up into a large high chamber. One could feel breezes as if the rock was porous.

The deeper we walked, the lighter it became, but it was impossible to tell from where the light entered.

The chamber narrowed and made a left turn; it became so narrow that Tony and I could not walk side by side; we had to walk single file.

Then the passageway widened again, but Tony stopped short so suddenly I tripped against him.

"We have company, Swede," he said.

I stepped past him and stared at the far wall of the chamber. I could hear Tony pull in his breath.

It was a huge bizarre wall painting of a woman in a long white robe.

She had the head of a cat.

"There's more of them, Swede! Look!" Tony whispered.

My eyes moved along the wall. There were sixteen such paintings. All of them alike except for the head. There was a different cat head on each painting.

"Let's get out of here, Swede, this is very spooky," Tony urged, pulling at my arm. I shook him off. My body was literally tingling from what I was looking at.

"Don't you know who you're looking at, Tony?"

"No."

"You are looking at Bast, the Egyptian goddess who was the personification of the gentle and life-giving heat of the sun. The cat was sacred to Bast and she is usually depicted cat-headed."

A hundred points of light seemed to be bursting in my head; a hundred memories. It was like a scroll being unraveled right in front of me.

"How many murders were there, Tony?" I asked.

"Seventeen."

"Right. But only sixteen paintings. The last two victims, the Tyre brothers, had only one cat. Seventeen victims, sixteen cats, sixteen paintings."

"What the hell are you talking about, Swede?"

I was becoming so excited I could hardly reply. Things were falling into place like a pinball machine. Disparate elements were joining. I had never felt such intellectual excitement in my life.

"Tony," I finally said, "walk over to the third painting."

"Why?"

"Just do it!"

He walked over to it, and even though there was light in the chamber, he lit two matches and held them together, stretching his arm high up along the painting.

"Do you know who you are looking at now?" I asked him, my voice quivering from the excitement I felt.

"A lady with the head of a cat."

"That's the face and head of Jill Bonaventura's white cat, Missy."

Tony snuffed out the matches and stepped back. He looked confused. Then he said, "Third painting, third victim, third cat."

"Right, Tony!"

Then he said, excited: "Then the last painting has to be a Siamese cat head because the two brothers had a Siamese cat." He started to turn in place, laughing and whooping like a banshee, the sounds echoing off the walls and assailing our ears. Suddenly he stopped acting stupid. He looked at me blankly. "But so what, Swede? What the hell does this mean?"

I ignored his question. And asked him: "Do you have any cash on you?"

"Sure."

"Then let's take a cab down to Retro."

"Anything you say, Swede."

Slowly, carefully, still dazed by the splendor, force, and perplexity of the wall paintings, we made our way out of the cave.

# 18

The ugly clock on the wall read 2:20 in the afternoon. Tony and I had now been waiting for Judy Mizener for more than two hours.

Tony was nervous and angry at being kept waiting. I really didn't mind it. I had a lot to think about ... to sift through. The finding of those remarkable cave paintings had been a massive shock to my nervous system. There was too much to think about. There were too many possibilities that had suddenly opened up. I was like a bloodhound that, after days of futile hunting in a forest which yields no scents, is suddenly given dozens of scent clues as the hunted's clothing begins to turn up piece after piece.

"Where did you work, Swede?"

"In a cubicle down the hall, near the computer room."

"This place is depressing."

I nodded in agreement and closed my eyes. The chair was uncomfortable. The cat goddess, Bast, kept popping in and out of my consciousness ... as if it was a fashion show ... with each reappearance on the runway assuming a different cat face.

Finally Judy Mizener came out of her office and stared balefully at both of us.

"I really am very busy," she said.

"It's important."

"And I prefer not to have ex-employees of Retro wandering around. Couldn't this have been done on the phone?"

"Not really," I said, standing up and holding my ground.

"Okay. Come in."

Tony and I walked into her small cramped office. One wall was piled high with different-color files.

I introduced Tony to her. She nodded and slid back behind her desk.

"Now, what can I do for you?" she asked.

I started to speak and then stopped. It was important to be careful. I had to get Judy Mizener into that cave now. But if I was to speak about an ancient sun goddess with the head of a cat painted on a cave in Central Park, she would think I was crazy. She had to see Bast herself—in the Cave . . . she had to see the faces of the victims' cats.

"We are very close to breaking the case," I said simply.

She stared at me, not answering, as if trying to evaluate my sanity, my honesty. Then she stared at Tony . . . up and down . . . as if evaluating him as an employee.

"Is that right?" she finally responded coolly, archly.

I pressed on. "We found some evidence ... the most important evidence that has been uncovered so far."

"Where is it?"

"It isn't portable. You'll have to come with us and bring a camera."

"What is it, specifically?"

"It's very hard to describe."

"Try."

"I'd rather not. I'd rather you came with us now."

She exploded. "Look! I can't just run out of my office every time someone comes in with a crazy scheme."

"You better go with us," Tony said quietly.

"Is your friend threatening me?" Judy asked me, startled.

"He's just being helpful."

The phone on her desk rang. She picked it up quickly and spoke a few words ... something about a computer run ... then slammed the receiver down.

"How long do you think it will take?" she asked me.

"We'll take a cab outside. Figure two hours."

She leaned back in her chair, picked up a pencil, and began to drum it on top of the phone. It was bizarre. I felt like a director trying to coax a great star to interpret a certain role with more precision. But I really didn't know enough about her personality to push the right buttons. Should I pray to the sun goddess Bast? Even more absurd. Why hadn't I made this woman my friend from the very beginning? Why hadn't Judy Mizener and I been friends?

Tony fixed the problem in a lunatic way. The strain of the scene was just too much for him, so he leapt up and went into one of his lunatic impersonations, this time of a Southern Baptist fire-and-brimstone preacher. "Sister," he yelled at Judy Mizener, "I'm gonna set you free . . . I'm gonna set you free . . . I'm gonna break the prison bars for thee." Judy Mizener stared at me as if my companion had gone crazy and I should control him. Then she just broke up into laughter, saying: "Okay. I'll come. Set me free!" Ten minutes later the three of us walked out of Retro, not exactly arm in arm, but together.

From the first moment Judy Mizener saw the wall painting of the ancient Egyptian sun goddess, she was mesmerized. She kept walking back and forth, then approaching the wall paintings, then moving away from them.

"I saw something like this in the Museum . . . in the Egyptian Wing. Am I right?" she asked.

"You saw an original. These are bizarre copies, done in pastel and chalk, by Jack Tyre," I replied.

"Who is this supposed to be?"

"An ancient Egyptian sun goddess—Bast."

"How did you find them?"

"Jack Tyre had an old lover who told me he used to come into Central Park on weekends with his Siamese cat and come to this cave. It was a long shot. I just decided to check it out because everything had come to a dead end."

"I thought you were no longer involved with this case."

"Just because you fired me from Retro doesn't mean I should abrogate my responsibilities."

"How do you know it was Jack Tyre? Can you be sure?"

"He came here. Who else could it be?"

"Why does each figure have a different cat's head? The rest of the goddess is uniform throughout."

"You tell me," I retorted.

She stared at the paintings, then wheeled swiftly toward me. "Are you telling me that . . . ?" She threw up her hands in disbelief. Then came back to her point. "Are you telling me what I think you are telling me?"

"Yes," I said emphatically, "the heads of the goddess correspond exactly to what we know of the cats of the victims. And the order is sequential. In chronological time."

"My God!" was all she could say, in a kind of desperate whisper. Then she carefully walked down the wall, staring at each figure in its turn.

There was a clattering noise. But it was only Tony dropping the flashlight that Judy Mizener had provided us after she agreed to come with us. He apologized.

"Then Jack Tyre knew all the victims," Judy

Mizener said. "And he drew each cat goddess after he killed each victim."

"Or before. Or a year after they died. I don't think we can find that out," I replied. "And it doesn't prove that Jack Tyre murdered all those people with all those kinds of weapons. Besides, he seemed to be a gentle man. It is hard to believe that he could strangle anyone." I was trying to be as analytical as possible. But I could not yet tell her what I really thought. Because that had to be explored ... that had to be validated.

She began to pace quickly back and forth in front of the wall—clearly agitated and clearly confused. Then she threw back her head and laughed crazily, forlornly. "What are we talking about?" she asked. "We don't know what the hell we are looking at. It's all still crazy. It doesn't mean anything. Do you understand what I'm saying, Alice? It's just a wall of strange drawings."

"Amen," echoed Tony.

"Do you know what kind of goddess Bast was?" I asked Judy Mizener.

"You mean other than being a goddess with the head of a cat? No, I don't know."

"She was a sun goddess."

"So what?"

"In ancient Egypt the sun was the reigning god. And it was the sun which guaranteed eternal life."

"I don't know what you're talking about," she replied.

"When an individual died in ancient Egypt, he

or she expected to be resurrected in the not-too-distant future—body and soul—and that could be accomplished only by the sun god . . . or those goddesses associated with the sun."

"And Bast was such a goddess?"

"Correct."

"Bast could help you live forever?"

"Exactly."

"What are you telling me? That all this murder and paintings and nonsense like toy mice are coming out of some kind of cult of the dead?"

"It could be. But whatever it is, your Retro won't be any help."

"It sounds like you're setting me up for something."

"Yes," I said forcefully, "I am setting you up. To solve this very ugly case."

"And how can we do that when we can't even know what all the pieces mean?"

"I think we can trap the killer."

"If he or she is not Jack Tyre."

"Exactly."

"How, Alice?"

"This cave is an important part of Central Park history. It was closed up in the late 1930's. Everyone thinks it has remained sealed. The only ones who knew it wasn't were a few derelicts, Jack Tyre and his cat, and maybe his murderer. I think if the murderer knows that the cave is going to be publicly opened, he or she will get very nervous and try to erase those paintings."

"But the cave isn't going to be opened."

"I know. But we can make believe."

"What's the point of that?"

"Then the murderer will hear a report on TV that the cave is about to be opened because there have been some dead chickens found nearby ... some remnants of animal sacrifice, which means some kind of voodoo cult may have gotten into the cave. Because of this, the cave will be opened and then resealed."

"But no such thing is happening."

"We can fake it."

"How?"

"Retro. As head of Retro you have access to all the TV reporters. They die for this kind of crime nonsense. You can call them in hush-hush and say that this voodoo cult may be implicated in several dismemberment homicides and that the Parks Department has given you permission to go ahead and open it. They report it. We wait and pick up the murderer."

"I can't do something like that. What about my credibility in the future? And we don't know if it will lure this mysterious figure out to the cave."

"It will. Believe me."

"I just can't do that," she replied in an anguished voice.

"It's our only chance, Judy. Someone is out there ... someone very ugly."

"Are you really telling me that the murderer of those seventeen people is out there and is so frightened at the disclosure of these crazy goddess wall paintings that he will risk his life to erase them?"

I didn't answer for a while. I couldn't tell her what I really believed because she wouldn't understand. Even I didn't understand it completely. Not yet.

It was time to do what I did best—act. It was time to envelop Judy Mizener in an emotional web she could not escape.

"Listen to me carefully, Judy. You go in, day after day, to Retro. You coordinate, you hire, you evaluate. Once in a very great while you come up with something substantial ... and another major crime is close to being solved. But you know and I know that these toy-mouse murders are choking your computers. They're the ugliest murders you have ... it's the most perplexing unsolved major crime case in the city and the newspapers don't even know it exists. And Retro drew a total blank, didn't it? Nothing was coughed up. Let's face it, Judy. I was the only one who was even close. I was the one who told you there was a correlation between the missing cats. So you fired me. And lo and behold, we find all the missing cats—don't we? On wall paintings of an Egyptian goddess. Do what I ask you. Please, Judy. I may be wrong. But there is a very good chance I am right. And if I am, you and Retro get the credit. Oh, I know you don't need to be redeemed for firing me. But if you break the case, then Retro becomes a force—a major force. And you along with it. You'll be able to do a lot of things you can't do now. You'll even be able to keep eccentric investigators on the consultant payroll. You have everything to gain and nothing to lose. And it's really our last chance to help those poor dead people rest in peace."

It was a good delivery. It was a powerful speech. It turned her into my little sister, as if I was giving her both profound and inspirational wisdom as to herself and the world. The joke being that she had done much better vis-à-vis the real world than I could ever hope to.

She stared at me, then at Tony, then for a long time at the wall paintings.

"Let's do it," she finally said in her best fake-professional voice.

An hour later, Tony and I sat at a deep back table in the All State Café on West Seventy-second Street. I was very tired but I was also very hungry. Tony was drinking a brandy. I had a stein of ale.

"They used to have a great tomato salad here," Tony said, studying the menu. I ordered a rare burger. He ordered a chicken-salad sandwich.

"I hope you know what you're doing, Swede," Tony said, a slight grin on his still-wounded face.

"What do you think?"

He thought for a while, twirling the bottom of his brandy glass. The restaurant was beginning to fill up.

"I don't think anymore, Swede. I'm back in the

theater, don't you remember? I exist now on sheer gall."

"What's bothering you, Tony?"

"You mean other than confusion and fatigue and frustration and unrequited love?"

"We're not really having an affair, Tony. We can't go to bed every twelve hours."

"An old-fashioned retort, Swede."

"I'm basically an old-fashioned woman, Tony."

"Right. And I'm Jimi Hendrix." He finished the brandy and ordered another one. When it came to the table, he sipped it and then said, "Tell me the truth, Swede. Do you really think someone will show up in response to the scam?"

"Yes."

"Who? The murderer?"

For some reason, at that moment I felt motherly toward Tony. I reached across the table and touched his cheek. He jumped back involuntarily, startled. Then he relaxed. "Well, Swede, an overwhelming show of affection. I'm touched." I smiled and sipped my ale. The hamburger and the chicken salad came. I slowly poured some catsup between the bun.

"What if I told you, Tony, that there might be no murderer?"

The sandwich halted before he reached his mouth.

"What?"

"You heard me."

"You mean all those people aren't dead?"

"Oh, they're dead, for sure."

"Well, what do you mean?"

I had said too much already. "Eat your sandwich, Tony. I have something more important to discuss with you."

He took a large bite of his sandwich, chewed it thoughtfully, swallowed, and then sipped his brandy.

"I have a feeling," he said, "that I'm about to be sent on another journey."

"Exactly."

"Can I finish my sandwich?"

"Of course. Then you go to see Billy Shea."

"Who is that?"

"The boy they first arrested for the Tyre murders. And after you talk to him I want you to rent another car and finish the trip that was so rudely interrupted—up to that garden spot of the Adirondacks called on the map Desolate Swamp."

"Swede, have mercy!"

"Oh, it won't be so bad this time. And besides, I'm going to write out complete instructions for you. I know how it is with you theater people . . . you have so many other things on your mind."

# 19

It was pouring. I stood under the umbrella at the corner of Canal and Broadway. It was seven-thirty in the morning, and I hadn't the slightest idea why Judy Mizener had asked me to meet her on a street corner rather than in the Retro offices.

She showed up fifteen minutes later and we went to a Chinese coffee shop just off Canal which sold those delicious sticky little meat buns.

"I did what you asked me," she said after we had sat down and been served our breakfast. Then she added, "With modifications."

She looked nervous and uncomfortable.

"What modifications?" I asked gently.

Suddenly she seemed to lose the whole train of our conversation. She blurted out: "I haven't been able to get over what I saw yesterday in that cave. I don't know why. They were just chalk paintings on a wall. But I kept dreaming about the cat goddess during the night. And I can't believe what I saw. I can't believe that each drawing had the head of a different cat. I can't believe they were the personification of the murdered people's cats! Do you understand me?"

I didn't answer. She sounded a bit hysterical. It was best to wait. I finished the bun. She calmed down and buried her face in her hands for a moment. It was a bit early in the morning to exhibit such total despair. Poor Judy Mizener.

"What modifications?" I repeated, trying to bring her back to the reality of our situation.

She sat up straight, as if showing me that she was now back in control. "First of all," she said, "the Parks Department won't participate in any such scam ... they want nothing to do with planting false media stories about something in one of their parks."

"But they won't interfere with you planting it?"

"Exactly. Second, I have decided to keep Retro's name out of it completely. Third, I'm going to contact only one network, Channel Nine News."

She waited for me to say something. I kept quiet. What she had said made me unhappy, but there was nothing I could do about it.

"I have an appointment with Channel Nine at eleven this morning. I just want to tell you what I'm going to say to them."

She sipped her coffee. The rain outside had stopped.

"Go ahead," I said.

"I'm going to make it very simple. A landmark cave near the lake in Central Park is going to be opened sixty years after it was sealed shut. Why? Animal remains about the cave seem to indicate that some type of strange animal-sacrific cult has penetrated the cave and is using it for illegal purposes. It is believed that several members of the cult are recently arrived Haitians. In Haiti, many of the voodoo cults have been implicated in murder-for-hire and drug smuggling. And that's all I'm going to tell them."

"I think that will be enough," I replied.

"Is it too outlandish for them to swallow?"

"No. Why should it be?"

"As you can see, Alice, I'm nervous. I'm taking a big chance for you."

"For me?"

"Well, it's your idea. And once in a while I get the feeling that you're about to make a fool out of me."

"Do you think I was the one who made those cave paintings?"

"Of course not. But I think you know a lot more than you're telling me."

"You're having second thoughts, aren't you, Judy?"

Her eyes flared at me. "I told you I'm going through with it."

"Thank you."

"Okay. Let's get down to the plan. It'll probably be broadcast over the ten o'clock news. If our killer sees it, he will move quickly. That's the way I see it."

"I agree."

"Of course ... that will happen only if you are right ... if those cave paintings are important enough so that their exposure will threaten him."

"Right."

"Now, I can't give you any backup, Alice. Are you going to stake out the cave alone?"

"No," I lied, "my friend Tony will be with me." There was no reason for me to tell her that Tony had left on a trip. She was already too uneasy.

"Do you have a permit for a weapon?"

"I don't." And then I lied again. "But Tony does. He has the permit and the weapon."

"Do you have a portable phone?"

"No."

"Then my suggestion is that you stay well away from the cave. If you see anything suspicious, just call 911 from one of the park phones. They're all over the Ramble."

The rain started again. Then there were thunderclaps. We sat together in the coffee shop, oddly silent, finishing our sweet rolls and coffee. For some reason I felt that I had known Judy Mizener for years.

Suddenly she stretched her hand across the table. I took it and held it.

"We both need luck," she said gently, smiling.

"Yes," I agreed, "we need a great deal of luck."

She left first. I left fifteen minutes later.

# 20

Bushy woke me by calmly walking over my head. I sat up quickly, in a panic, and stared at the clock. Then I sank back on the bed. It was only three o'clock in the afternoon. The newscast on TV would go on at ten in the evening. I didn't have to go into the park until then—at the earliest.

My fears were beginning to emerge. Would the TV plant do its job? Would he or she show up? Was the disclosure of those cave paintings really so crucial to this hidden person? Would I be safe in the park?

I had come to one very intelligent conclusion: I would *not* under any circumstance try to apprehend the intruder if the intruder showed. After all, I was not physically violent. I had no weapon. And all I needed to confirm or explicate or bring the whole horrendous mess to a conclusion was a face or a name. If the intruder was not known by me, I could remember enough to produce a sketch and Judy Mizener and the police could do the rest.

When everything becomes precarious in my life, I start to clean the apartment. And that was

what I did at four o'clock. Luckily, I despise vac-
uum cleaners so I spent two lovely hours pushing
an absurd carpet sweeper back and forth picking
up the cat hairs. As usual, it was a rather futile
endeavor. The carpet sweeper picked nothing up.
It merely moved the cat hairs and other debris
into readily accessible piles, which I then picked
up by hand. At seven in the evening I ate one
hard-boiled egg, one piece of cheese, one banana,
and one stale strawberry tart.

At eight in the evening the panic came over
me again. What if my analysis of the murders
had been wrong? Why hadn't I confided in anyone? Why had I kept it to myself? Was I that
arrogant that I didn't need confirmation or criti-
cism? A lot had suddenly become clear to me
when I discovered those bizarre wall paintings
... but my comprehension and analysis could
have been colored by the lingering grudge I held
against Retro for firing me. Why did I persist in
keeping it within me ... as if it were some kind
of secret treasure?

Time moved very slowly. It enveloped me. At
nine o'clock I started to tremble a bit and it was
hard to breathe. Stage fright? I burst out laughing. I hadn't felt that bad since I was about to
appear in my first stage performance in St.
Paul—at the old Tyrone Guthrie Regional Theater.

My grandmother had come to see me from her
dairy farm. She saw my state. She told me that
when she was nervous she read her Bible. What

Bible, Grandma? I asked her. And she shyly and slyly took out an old book and gave it to me. It wasn't a Bible. It was a book called *Bird-Watching in Florida*. It was the fantasy life of an old woman on a frigid Minnesota dairy farm who thought she would one day spend a few weeks in Florida looking for exotic birds. She never made it. I hadn't looked at it that night long ago in St. Paul. But why shouldn't I look at it now?

I found it fifteen minutes later in my hall closet, buried beneath some old scrapbooks. Its green cover was battered and stained. Grandma's name was still visible, printed in red ink. That I remembered well; she always used red ink in a leaky old-fashioned fountain pen.

I opened the book at random. It read:

Bonaparte's gull. *Larus philadelphia*. This small, strikingly patterned gull flies into Florida during fall and winter. The head is black in the breeding season, but white with a black spot when immature, and in winter. But on its swift flight over foamy wave tops, white outer primaries flash snowy by its gray mantle, unmistakably.

The reading did nothing for my fears. I checked the clock. Nine-thirty. I dressed quickly: half-boots, black knit sweater, black corduroy pants. I pulled my long hair up into a small bun and capped it with a ski cap. It was spring, but the park must be chilly at night.

I decided to wait for the news program and

then rush to the park in a cab. At ten o'clock I turned the program on.

At ten-twenty they broadcast the story. The announcer used Judy Mizener's words, exactly as she had told it to me in the coffee shop. Then they showed a stock photo of the cave. I couldn't tell if it was the cave in question or some other one.

Then the announcer gave the kicker: the cave would be opened the following day to determine if it had been used by violent voodoo-type cults, and then resealed. Then the weather man came on.

I left the apartment quickly, walked to Third Avenue, and took a cab up to Fifty-seventh and Seventh. I entered the park at Fifty-ninth and Seventh and headed toward the bow bridge, which provided access to the Ramble. It was the first time in my life I had ever been in Central Park at night—but there were many people about, joggers and walkers and cars and bicyclists.

The moment, however, I crossed the bridge, I entered a quiet darkness. Where were the homeless I had seen before? Were they on the wooded slopes? I walked quickly, head down, at the point where the path met the grass.

It was not hard to find the cave this time. Even in the darkness the path was etched in my head like a compass. I located the slope; I climbed it easily; I slipped through the narrow opening.

Once inside, using a pocket flashlight, I moved

swiftly through the cave until I reached the high vaulted chamber where the wall paintings were located. At night, as well as during the day, there were slivers of light that seemed to filter in from above. But all these slivers could do was pierce the gloom haphazardly. One could not truly see without a flash or a match.

I slouched down against the far wall, totally hidden from humans and bats and ghosts.

All was in place. The lights were down. The curtain was about to be raised. The stagehands were nervously out of sight, wherever they may be. The ushers had moved to the lobby. The audience was slowly twirling their rolled-up programs in their hands. The players were beginning to lose their stage fright and feel the rush of adrenaline.

I checked my watch. It was only five minutes to eleven. It had taken me a mere thirty minutes to arrive here, from the moment I stepped out of my apartment.

An hour passed. My slouch cramped my legs, so I stretched out in a sitting position, my back against the wall. The ground was damp and I had forgotten to bring a mat or a pillow or even an extra sweater to sit on. I could feel flashes of those bizarre paintings through the haphazard filtered light. Where was the light coming from? Moonlight? Streetlights that lined the path with the iron railing over the top half of the cave? I didn't know.

The minutes and then the hours slipped by. I

dozed and then stirred. It wasn't really sleep—it was a kind of numbing unconsciousness.

It was past three when I heard that first chilling sound. A kind of crunch, a distance away.

I pulled my feet up to my face, almost in a fetal position, hoping, cowardly, that it was just a creature or the wind.

And then the crunch was repeated. Someone was walking in the cave toward the chamber.

My heart was pounding so hard I thought it would burst through my rib cage.

The entrance to the chamber clouded over. Someone was in front of the wall paintings! My eyes could make out a shrouded form.

I saw a glint of something ... an object ... and then a sound like water being poured from a bucket. My eyes could make out something being sprayed along the wall. I understood then what was happening. The individual was using spray paint to obliterate the paintings. The glint was the side of an aerosol can.

Then the figure turned and started to leave the chamber. I had seen nothing. I could identify no one. It wasn't supposed to happen like this. Not at all. The whole project was becoming futile. I had to see who it was.

I panicked. Without thinking about my safety ... without considering anything but the fact that I simply could not remain hidden while the solution slipped away in darkness ... I stood up and cried out: "Arcenaux!"

The figure froze at the entrance of the chamber. Then he turned toward me ... the face of red-haired Detective Arcenaux suddenly visible.

"You stupid, prying bitch!" he cried out, and strode toward me, his weapon in hand.

I ran for the opening. He tripped me up and I sprawled over the ground. When I turned over, his gun was inches away from my face.

Everything happened so fast then. I heard a shout from behind us.

Then a body smashed against Arcenaux's face. The gun fell to the ground.

Arcenaux rolled over, holding his hands up to protect his face.

I sat up. Straddling Arcenaux was a tiny man, his powerful arms and shoulders keeping the detective immobilized. It was Bert Turk!

"What is going on here?" another voice called. Judy Mizener was standing there, running a large beamed flashlight over the wall paintings, which had now been covered over by red spray paint.

She approached us. Bert Turk rolled off Arcenaux, breathing heavily.

"You really didn't think I would let you do this alone, did you?" she asked, helping me to my feet.

"In fact, I did," I admitted, standing unsteadily.

Judy Mizener stared at Arcenaux. "What are you doing here?" He didn't answer. She turned back to me, perplexed. "Does he have something to do with this whole mess?"

"Yes, he does."

"You mean one of our own detectives is the Toy Mouse Murderer?"

"Oh, no, Judy. Arcenaux is no murderer. He's worse. He was a consultant, a courier, a concierge of death. He was implicated in every murder. He advised every murderer."

"Every murderer? How many were there?"

"Seventeen victims. Sixteen murderers. And one suicide—the last, Jack Tyre."

"Alice, you've had a scare. Go slow now. Think before you talk. You're not making much sense." Judy Mizener placed a consoling hand on my arm. I shook it off.

"Do you remember that Jonestown horror?" I asked.

"Of course. A mass suicide. The religious cult that extinguished itself—about eight hundred people, mostly Americans—in Guyana, by drinking poisoned Kool-Aid."

"Well, what we're dealing with is very much the same—only on a smaller and more exotic scale. Jack Tyre was a charismatic man, a visionary who did not hesitate to proselytize for his vision. He preached a very ancient Egyptian creed."

I was calm. I was in control. It was like I was watching my analysis unfold and marveling at its lucidity. Yet, only minutes before I had been groveling on the wet ground in fear.

"The creed of Bast?" Judy Mizener asked.

"Yes, but with his own slight modifications. Jack Tyre obviously believed that this life was only an ugly preview of the glory to come in the next life. That the believer would be resurrected in the next life, body and soul. That the ideal mode in which to enter eternal life was as a cat. He gathered about himself cat lovers who were fascinated by Egyptian lore. They spent hours together among the artifacts of the Egyptian collection at the Metropolitan Museum of Art.

"Jack Tyre's pseudo-Egyptian gospel was powerful. And he spoke—in the eyes of his followers—with the authority of Bast, the sun goddess who traditionally conferred immortality with the gentle rays of the sun. Lovely cat-headed Bast—the emblem of the sun god who brought new life to the dead just as the new plants came up in the fields.

"Tyre created the scenario. His followers should not prolong their entry into paradise. Probably they drew lots to begin their demonic journey. Victim number one was murdered by victim number two. Victim number two was murdered by victim number three . . . and so on."

Judy pleaded, "Go slower, Alice. Go slower."

I breathed deeply in and out, then continued: "The moment a victim died, his or her cat was shipped to a desolate area of the Adirondacks to live out its life as a feral cat under the supposed guidance of the sun goddess. The moment the cat died of natural causes in the wild, the victim would enter the gates of paradise resurrected as the cat he or she loved."

"It is all so crazy," Judy Mizener muttered.

Fatigue suddenly broke into my clarity. My head was beginning to spin. I leaned against the wall for support.

"That was why the sequence of the murders always mimicked the fertility and birth cycles of the cat. The believers were about to be reborn into eternal life as cats."

Arcenaux made a sudden movement. Bert Turk turned the detective's own gun on him. "Keep him quiet," Judy Mizener told the small man. Then she asked me, "What was the toy mouse about?"

"It wasn't left for the cat. It was left for the human. The Egyptians always provided gifts for the dead on their journey to the next life. The toy mouse was a symbolic gift signifying the transfer from human to divine cat. That's what the crooked pictures were all about also. They signified that this life was crooked ... ugly ... deranged."

"But how is Arcenaux tied to all this—concretely?"

"Each member of this cult contributed twenty-five hundred dollars a year—a kind of tithe ... a membership fee in the church of Bast. That money was paid to Arcenaux in exchange for him helping them execute the ritual murders cleanly. Only a homicide detective could have been able to ingeniously create a different M.O. for each murder—a different weapon for each divine assassination. In fact, only the lucky hunch about the toy mouse spoiled the plan. Arcenaux was also used to transport the cats to the Adirondacks. But only Jack Tyre knew of Arcenaux's connection with the plot. He was Arcenaux's control. He gave the detective the money each year. Arcenaux reported only to Tyre."

"How did you piece all this together, Alice?"

"It turns out that Arcenaux helped conduct the investigation into Jill Bonaventura's murder many years ago. He interviewed her brother, who must have told him about the twenty-five hundred dollars he gave his sister each year—not knowing what it was for. But that information was never entered into the Retro files by Arcenaux. He also slipped up once in a moment of sadness and told me that his great ambition in life was to own a trucking firm. At the time, I thought it was his attempt at a humorous statement. His participation in the crimes was made clearer and more precise to me after the attempted murder of Tony Basillio on his trip upstate to check out an important lead. At first I thought that Karl Bonaventura was the shooter. But after he committed suicide the day before Tony went up there, I realized it had to be someone at Retro. Only people with access to the computer knew I had been to Jill Bonaventura's apartment, where I found the slip showing that Jill was about to ship her cat to the Desolate Swamp in the Adirondacks in accordance with the cult's belief that the cat must die in the feral state."

Judy Mizener walked slowly over to Arcenaux.

She seemed to find it difficult to absorb—or believe—what I had told her. She seemed alternately reluctant and then happy to believe it.

"Tell me, John," she asked gently, "why did you deface these paintings?"

Arcenaux didn't answer. Judy Mizener persisted. "Is what she is saying true? Did it happen that way, John?"

Detective John Arcenaux persisted in his silence. Judy Mizener turned back to me.

"Do you have any hard proof of all this ... of Arcenaux's complicity? Obliterating wall paintings is not really a crime."

"Tony will have that evidence for you in a few hours. As soon as he comes back from upstate. As for Arcenaux's motives. Money, no doubt. Over the years he must have collected almost two hundred thousand dollars in annual dues from the cult members. Of course, each year, the contributions were reduced by twenty-five hundred as another member entered paradise. But I think it was more than just the money. There was the perverse challenge. And maybe not a little madness. Who knows? Maybe he just liked being around a very strange group of people. Maybe he's a sort of cult groupie."

"Those people were lunatics."

"No, Judy, you have it wrong. Their beliefs were as valid and as authentic as any other belief system. In fact, their faith was quite beautiful. I would like to believe that this life is only a pale, ugly preview of something to come. And I surely would like to spend eternity in the guise of a cat goddess."

"Do I cuff him?" Bert Turk suddenly asked, staring at Arcenaux with profound distaste.

"Why not?" Judy Mizener replied. "We'll book him on disorderly conduct and defacing park property. At least until we can get a conspiracy indictment on the murders."

Wearily we filed out of the cave.

# 21

I stared into the white foam of my cappuccino. We were in a coffee shop on Madison Avenue and Thirty-seventh Street in Manhattan. Tony was seated across from me. He was drinking his. Then he put the cup down with a theatrical gesture . . . as if the beverage was something he had been given for great heroism . . . as if it was a gift.

"I gave everything to Mizener. You were absolutely right, Swede. There was a small trucking company up near Desolate Swamp with Arcenaux listed as one of the partners. No one up there gave me any trouble. Your Retro identification card opened all kinds of doors for me. He also has a bank account upstate, and two CD's."

"What amounts?"

"They total about a hundred and seventy-three thousand."

"Not a lot when you consider it represents consultant fees in seventeen murders."

"Was it the money, Swede? Was that why Arcenaux did it?"

"I don't know. Maybe he doesn't know."

"And you were right about that kid, Swede—about Billy Shea. He was paid to get the cat out of the Tyres' apartment. Just like that neighborhood kid who grabbed Jill Bonaventura's cat out of her apartment. The trouble is, Billy Shea can't I.D. Arcenaux. He told me the man who dealt with him wore big dark glasses."

"Well, let Judy Mizener sort it out."

"Do you know how Arcenaux got involved in the beginning? I mean, he doesn't have a cat. And he doesn't seem like the kind of guy who is obsessed with ancient Egyptian theology."

"I discovered that Arcenaux's first assignment in the NYPD was as a mounted cop in Central Park. That's where he probably met Jack Tyre. Tyre needed someone who knew weapons."

Tony sat back and stretched. Then he shook his head slowly from side to side, incredulously.

"Swede," he said, "tell me about those people. I mean, tell me why they did it."

"You mean why they believed what they believed?"

"I mean ... to the point of ending their lives suddenly ... of their own free will."

"Many people yearn for immortality. Many people believe this life is worthless. There have been a lot stranger cults."

"But, Swede ..."

"Don't get me wrong, Tony. I'm not apologizing for what they did. But it is an elegant concept—to live forever in the bodies of the creatures they love the most."

"A cat is a cat, Swede."

"No, Tony. A cat is ... in a lonely harsh world ... the repository of what is left of beauty and grace and truth."

Suddenly my effusive words embarrassed me. I changed the subject abruptly.

"I have to go on a cat-sitting assignment now, just a few blocks from here. How about coming along?"

"Why not? It's better than the Adirondacks."

We left the coffee shop and walked slowly to Mrs. Salzman's apartment. We held hands as we walked, like children.

On the way, I told him about Abelard. And I told him that since this was my last visit to Mrs. Salzman, I was determined to finally flush Abelard out and see him.

Once inside, I saw that Mrs. Salzman had left me a lovely good-bye note in the kitchen, attached to my pay envelope. I put them both into my purse.

"Where is the beast?" Tony asked.

"Somewhere in the apartment. We have to listen and then corner him. Abelard is very elusive. But sometimes you can hear him under the furniture."

We walked slowly through the apartment, listening. We heard nothing.

"Are you sure there's a cat in this apartment?" Tony asked.

"Don't be stupid. Of course there is." I pulled Tony first to the food dish and then to the litter box—both of which showed evidence that a cat lived in the apartment. "Abelard just doesn't like to reveal himself," I explained.

"Why?"

"I don't know."

Suddenly Tony held his finger up to his lips, cautioning silence.

A second later he slammed his hand down on a table! It sounded like an explosion.

Then we clearly heard a scurrying under the furniture. It was Abelard!

Tony walked forward. I followed. He slammed his hand down again on a piece of furniture. We heard Abelard scurrying away from the sound again.

It was obvious what Tony was doing—he was driving poor Abelard into a corner with the loud sounds ... like a sheepdog yaps at a flock of sheep.

We kept moving down the hallway and finally cornered him in the alcove between the end of the hall and the living room—under a divan.

"We've got him now," Tony said gleefully. "I'll pick up the divan. You grab your friend."

How I longed to finally see and hold Abelard! Tony started to lift the divan.

"Wait!" I called out. He stared at me, confused. "What's the matter, Swede? I thought you wanted to get this cat."

I turned away. Suddenly it dawned on me that I didn't want to see poor Abelard. I found myself frightened by the bizarre possibility that when

the divan was raised, I would not see Abelard—
I would see Bast! I would see Bast rising off the
floor in her cat-headed glory.

"Leave him!" I said to Tony urgently. My back
was wet with perspiration. We walked quickly
out of the apartment as if pursued by demons.

Once on the street, Tony said, "I think I got a
glimpse of him, Swede. He had two ears, two
eyes, one nose, four paws, and a tail. A very
handsome cat indeed."

I wasn't listening to his quip. I wanted to get
back to my apartment quickly, where I could
avoid all things Egyptian for a while. I was safe
there. I mean, even if I was reincarnated in feline
form, it wouldn't be as Bushy or Pancho. They
were just too difficult.

# 22

The police officer blocked my way. He was burly. He said nastily: "No I.D.—no access! It's as simple as that, lady."

"I don't have an I.D. card. I don't work for Retro anymore. Judy Mizener told me to come in and pick up some stuff I had forgotten to take."

I explained the situation to him like he was a child. I was furious at myself for coming to Retro again. But Judy Mizener had called me and said there was a whole batch of stuff in my cubicle that I had forgotten to clear out. She asked me to take it away as quickly as possible.

At the mention of those magic words—Judy Mizener—the officer got on the phone.

Ten seconds later he stepped aside, allowing me to enter the sacred precincts. I walked quickly to the small cubicle.

There was a typed note fastened to the outside panel of the cubicle. It read:

Alice:
  We moved your stuff to the north meeting room. Please pick it up there.

Judy Mizener

P.S. Arcenaux wants to plead guilty to obstruction-of-justice and income-tax-evasion charges in return for our dropping the conspiracy/murder charge. No decision yet. Take care of yourself.

I crumpled the note and left it on the empty desk. I walked to the meeting room. There was no desire on my part to meet any Retro staff. Anyway, the halls were empty ... the staff just wasn't about.

I stepped into the meeting room, closed the door behind me, and reached for the light switch on the wall.

Something grabbed my wrist in an iron lock!

I screamed in the darkness.

Suddenly the room was flooded with light.

I found myself staring at this enormous white face.

It was only inches away.

My legs were trembling. My heart was thumping in my chest. I stepped back.

Then I realized that I was staring at a mouse face.

I was staring at the face and body of a huge white mouse balloon that seemed to fill the entire room.

A second later it vanished with an enormous bang.

There was Judy Mizener, grinning, a shiny hat pin in her hand—the weapon that had punctured the toy.

Suddenly the room filled up with people. There was Bert Turk and Rothwax and virtually the entire staff of Retro, including the computer operators.

They started to clap and it took me many dazed moments before I realized that they were clapping for me ... and that the huge white mouse balloon toy had been their gift to me ... their apology to me ... and ultimately their tribute to me for a job well done.

"I think we deserve a speech," Judy Mizener said, holding up her hand for silence and then pulling me toward the center of the room.

There were cans of beer and bottles of whiskey on the table in front of the blackboard, along with small sandwiches and Danish and a host of paper plates and cups. The whole thing was bizarre and touching. It was a surprise party for *me*.

I looked around the room. They were all waiting for me to speak. There were no catcalls now.

For the first time in my life, I was speechless. A thousand parts and I couldn't remember one line.

Still, they waited patiently.

Finally I recited the only thing I could remember right then—the Mother Goose nursery rhyme about the crooked man who bought a crooked cat which caught a crooked mouse and they all lived together in a little crooked house.

Don't miss Alice Nestleton's
next mystery adventure

# A Cat by Any Other Name

coming from Signet in May 1992!

# 1

There were three Siamese kittens. Winken was on my head. Blinken was playing with my right thumb. And the third, Nod, was on the carpet in front of me, staring up at me with her profoundly sad eyes.

A second later they all changed places and I couldn't tell who was who.

The night was warm. The glass doors of the terrace were open and I could see out over the East River and the lights of the Queensborough Bridge. Ava Fabrikant's Sutton Place apartment was magnificent; it nestled like a jewel in the ivy-covered building, twenty-three stories above the river.

We had eaten the orange duck and now we were all waiting for the Great Moment. There was Ava and her husband, Les. Barbara Roman and her husband, Tim. Sylvia Graff and her gentle alcoholic husband, Pauly. Renee Lupo and myself.

What was the Great Moment?

The serving of peppermint tea.

Oh, not just any tea! But tea brewed from the first crop to come up in our community herb garden on the Lower East Side of Manhattan. Fifteen tiny green peppermint leaves.

Three months before, one of my cat-sitting clients had told me about four women, all cat lovers, who were going to create an herb garden on a tiny parcel of wretched, garbage-strewn land, just off Avenue B. They were, she told me, going to plant basil and coriander and dill and thyme and chamomile and peppermint. And, above all, they were going to plant catnip and catamint. Then, along with school children from the area, they were going to harvest and dry the herbs, package them, and sell them to gourmet food stores—with all the proceeds going to the ASPCA.

It struck me as romantic and quixotic: An herb garden in the city?

But why not? I hadn't dug into the earth since I left my grandmother's dairy farm to go to the big city almost twenty-five years ago. And I needed a change in my life. I needed something different—nontheatrical—basic.

So I called and they welcomed me. The last three months of planning and planting and fertilizing a small desolate patch of urban earth had been glorious.

Barbara Roman sat down on the sofa beside me. Winken, Blinken, and Nod immediately switched their allegiance and overran her. Her laughter came in peals. She picked Blinken up with one hand and held the kitten close to her face.

"I wonder," she said, "what Swampy would make of you"—Swampy was her grizzled old Tom cat. Then she kissed Blinken on the nose. That was too much and off the kitten flew, the other kittens following. Five seconds later they were out of sight.

The sounds of gentle bickering over the brewing process wafted into the living room from Ava's immense kitchen. "Hell hath no fury like middle-aged herb gardeners," Barbara noted.

I laughed. I was beginning to pick up a faint odor of peppermint. I turned to Barbara to tell her but she had already picked it up and was nodding happily. We were very much in synch.

Barbara was the first good friend I had made in twenty years. We spent hours on the phone together. She was interested in me: in my acting, in my cat sitting, in my crime solving, in the men who had shared my life. Barbara was literate and witty—but above all she had the gift of compassion. I was not the only person who thought that. Everyone who knew this small brown-haired woman with a penchant for smocks loved her. Even if they didn't, they listened to her because she made sense. Maybe she was, in the old-fashioned sense, wise.

She leaned over toward me. "Look at poor Renee." I looked across the room where Sylvia Graff's husband, Pauly, was telling her some kind of disjointed story. Barbara speculated, "Renee is making believe she's listening but her mind is on the peppermint tea."

Then a shout of triumph came from the kitchen and Ava appeared, holding a tray. On the tray were eight tiny Japanese tea cups.

"Drum roll, please!" she shouted at her husband, Les, who did his best by slamming a fork against a piece of furniture.

Walking gingerly, as if she were carrying a priceless treasure, Ava approached the French Provincial dining table and carefully put the tray down.

We all rushed to the table. Each of us picked up a cup and held it high.

"Wait!" Les called out, "What about sugar?" He was greeted with such looks of withering scorn that he seemed to crunch down into the carpet.

"A toast is definitely in order," Sylvia said.

"To the plant we plucked the leaves from," Renee offered.

It was a lovely toast. We drank the tea. (There were only two fingers' worth in each cup.) After the Great Moment was over we placed the cups back onto the tray. No one knew what to say.

"Well," Ava finally said, "mine tasted like peppermint tea." We all burst out laughing. There are few things as ludicrous as searching for superlatives when they just don't apply.

After the tea we had a delicious lemon mousse, strong French Roast coffee and brandy.

The hours flew by. No one made any move to leave. At around eleven-thirty I found myself listening to Renee Lupo. Barbara stood next to me, sipping brandy. Behind her was Ava, holding a coffee cup.

"I read this fascinating article about trap gardening," Renee said.

"What is trap gardening?" Ava asked, adding, "It sounds almost cruel."

Barbara handed me her brandy glass to hold. "I'll be right back. I want to get some air."

"Well," Renee continued, "imagine that you are growing potatoes. But each year you've tried to grow them in the past, they've been decimated by potato beetles. What do you do if you're an organic gardener and refuse to use pesticides?"

"Pray?" asked Ava.

"No, you plant eggplant."

"Instead of the potatoes?" I asked, confused.

"No, in addition to the potatoes. You see, there is only one crop potato beetles like better than potatoes—and that is eggplant. So, the beetles will decimate the eggplant and leave the potatoes alone." Renee's dark eyes flashed. She was a writer and very intense. She saw cosmic significance in the most mundane of things. . . .

"What is that noise?" Ava asked. There was a noise now, a growing sound of horns.

Les called out from the far side of the room. "There must be a backup on the East River Drive. Take a look out, Ava."

Ava handed me her coffee cup. I now had Barbara's brandy glass in one hand and Ava's coffee cup in the other. She walked out onto the terrace. I looked for a place to put the glass and the cup. . . .

A horrible scream shattered the air around us! It seemed to suck the air from the room.

It came from the terrace.

We ran out and saw Ava standing by the terrace ledge. Her hands were cupping her face. The scream lingered on, gurgling in her throat.

I stared down, out over the railing. The cars were backed up as far as the eye could see in both directions. Their headlights glowed like circular fireflies.

On the highway, far below, lay a small black object.

It was a body.

We all looked around, furtively at first, then with increasing desperation.

Barbara Roman was not among us.

I looked at my hand. It was trembling. It still held the brandy glass. I walked slowly to the terrace wall and leaned against the brick so I wouldn't fall.

Barbara had handed me her brandy glass, walked out to the terrace, and leaped to her death.

Lydia Adamson is the pseudonym of
a well-known mystery writer.